# Consecrated Crime

## A JESSAMY WARD MYSTERY

PENELOPE CRESS, STEVE HIGGS

# Contents

# Rude Awakening

"Aunt Cindy, why are you dragging me out at this ungodly hour?" I stumbled behind her, bleary of eye and short of temper. It was mere minutes past five in the morning.

"Darling, you will see. Dave called me out, but I think this is something you can handle now." My aunt scurried up the path to the cottage hospital.

"Handle what? Why did the Baron call you and why are we heading to the hospital?" The Baron was my sister's pet name for her beau, Chief Inspector Dave Lovington.

"To talk with its latest guest!" Cindy paused momentarily outside the main entrance. The sun rising slowly across the eastern ridge behind her cast a golden sheen over her silver tresses. "Dave suspects it's a suicide, which, of course, is his usual default given what happened to his poor wife."

I froze. "Did you just say suicide?" I turned to head back to the comfort of my duvet. "I can't talk to the dead! I'm going home."

Cindy grabbed my fleeing arm and pulled me back. "I think you can. Suicide, accident or murder, this poor child's spirit will be desperate to have their voice heard. The possibilities to make a connection will be stronger than ever!"

"Cindy! I'm the local vicar. Church of England. Boring, straight-laced Protestant vibes only. No communing with the dead on my watch. Do you understand?"

Cindy refused to let go of my arm, no matter how hard I tried to wriggle free. "Come, darling, Dave is already downstairs. I can't keep him waiting."

"Does he know I am joining you for your little seance?" I knew from my aunt's sudden interest in the etched glazing of the hospital door that he did not. "That's it then, I'm going home."

"Don't you do last rites or something?" she countered.

"That's the other lot. The Catholics." To my aunt, all Christian denominations merged into one. "I'll offer some prayers of comfort for their family, which I can do at home."

Cindy's hand loosened. "Okay, I understand," she croaked. A rare tear dropped from her cheek.

"Aunt, what's wrong? There's something you're not telling me." I leaned against the door and tried to position myself to see her face better in the half-light.

"Jess, I can't do this alone." My aunt wiped another tear from the end of her nose with her sleeve. "It's the nature of things. As your power grows, mine weakens. Please come with me. Together, perhaps, we can give Dave some answers. Help him determine the cause of death."

"I'm sorry, I don't understand. There will be an autopsy, right?" The Inspector had warned me off his investigations so many times before. "You know my relationship with Dave is, well, strained. What with him dating my sister, and him being the Chief Inspector, and all the times I've gotten involved, even *solved* his murder cases. I'm not sure he would appreciate my poking about in another mysterious death on the island." My protests bounced off her unused tears now frozen into a recomposed, more obstinate stare. I had one last salvo in my arsenal. "He called you in. He wants your magical insight, not my nosey beak getting in the way."

"She washed up on the same beach," Cindy replied as if that revelation would counter all the above objections. My continued confusion forced her to carry on. "The same beach they found April on all those years ago." Maybe it was the lack of sleep, but I was still perplexed. "April? His late wife."

"Ah!" The penny finally dropped. "Oh."

"Yes."

"I see."

"Indeed."

"Okay," *Darn it!* I had no option but to play along. "But for the record, I think this is total madness."

"Duly noted." Cindy reached into her jacket pocket and pulled out a small jar of Vicks vapour rub. "Rub some of this under your nose. It will help with the smell."

\*\*\*

The temporary morgue beneath the Cottage Hospital was, as one would suspect, a sterile white box with strip lighting and several electric air fresheners plugged into the wall sockets. The Inspector was talking to Dr Sam Hawthorne when we arrived. Though Sam was my best friend, I had learnt that she always remained professional whilst on duty. There would be few clues to what she thought of this charade on her public countenance. I would have to wait until later over a drink at the vicarage, when I was sure she would have plenty to say.

"Cynthia, thank you for coming." Dave, ever the gentleman, especially to my ethereal maiden aunt, held out his hand to greet hers. He raised her hand to his lips and kissed her knuckles. His quizzical amber eyes shot a dart to me, then back to my aunt, then to me again. "Ah, Reverend Ward. Er? This is a pleasant surprise."

"Dave, darling. Jess is here to help me." *Well, that's cleared everything up then.* "Now, where have you stored this poor soul?"

Sam levered a silver hinge on the far wall and pulled out a metal gurney. The refrigeration unit pumped out a blast of cold air. I shivered.

"Are you sure Jess is ready for this?" Dave whispered to my aunt.

"I have seen dead people before, you know!" I stepped forward in defiance and pulled back the sheet covering the body. *But I have never seen a drowned one before!* My mouth filled with the remains of yesterday's aubergine bake. "Excuse me..."

I don't remember my best friend following me to the toilet, but I knew it was her pulling at the paper roll and reaching around to wipe my lips.

"Thank you." I steadied myself on the pedestal and turned around.

"That's what friends are for." Sam washed her hands. "Not what you expected, eh?"

"It was just a shock. Do we know who she is? Was?"

"No idea." Sam hit the button on the electronic dryer. "There was no I.D. on the body," she shouted over the hot air. "The coroner will be here on the first ferry. I don't really understand what Dishy Dave expects to achieve by calling in your aunt, *or* you. I didn't see that coming."

"Cindy says her powers are weakening, and she needs me." I splashed my face with cold water and caught my weary reflection in the mirror. "I'm not sure what she expects me to do."

Sam, in true 'jolly hockey sticks' style, slapped my back. "Game on then. Let's find out!"

The second time around, I kept the contents of my stomach where they belonged. Sam explained that from the state of decomposition, the victim had been in the water a day or two at most. "Without an autopsy, I can't confirm how she died, but there is a lot of damage to her body, which suggests she met with some rocks or a boat's motor on the way to the shore. But I can confirm she's female, probably in her twenties."

"Jess, we will take a hand each and see what we can see." Cindy gathered the corpse's right hand in both palms and closed her eyes. I took what remained of her left wrist and fingers, noting the lack of thumb. *There's no thumb!* Swallowing hard on a heady mix of cold air and vapour rub, I quietened my mind.

"Helen." Cindy softly whispered, "No, apologies, her name is Ellen. Ellen Finley?"

"Findlay," I answered. "Ellen Findlay."

*Oh my goodness!* Her voice was in my head. Young. Scottish. Scared

"She was on a boat. A yacht."

"Maybe a boat in the Regatta." Dave's trusty pencil scratched in his notebook.

"There are lots of little lights dotted around. I can hear the water lapping at the side of the boat." The dark harbour bobbed in the distance. There was a faint sound of music from a nearby yacht. Echoes of distant conversations. "It must be the Regatta."

"What boat are they on?" Dave asked.

Cindy replied. "She can't remember. It was an old-fashioned name. A woman's name."

"Not a great help." He muttered, "People often name their boats after women." Dave grew frustrated. "Anything else? Was it an accident?"

"She's not sure. She can't remember. There are lots of loud bangs. Fireworks? She's frightened." Fear gripped my heart. "Am I dead? She doesn't know she's dead!" I snatched my hands away.

Cindy leaned over Ellen's body and pulled herself close. "It's time, darling child. Time to move on. Walk towards the light, my dear." Taking a deep breath, Cindy straightened herself up. "Sam, do you have any hand sanitiser?"

*****

Breakfast back at the vicarage was a sombre affair. Mum had recently completed the sale of her house and most of her boxed belongings, and much of her furniture, bulged from every room on the ground floor awaiting its new home. Rosie was planning to take some of it to the cottage on Love Lane, and the rest would move with Mum to her new house. She had found a cute bungalow off the

Wesberrey Road with a garden that backed straight onto the beach. Until she had finalised all the paperwork on that purchase, and the agents handed over the keys, it would be like living in a junk shop. Our collective nerves were fraying. Talk of dead bodies in the morgue did little to cheer us up.

"I'll be honest," Dave piped in over a plate of vegetarian sausages, eggs and mushrooms, "I had hoped for more concrete evidence to go on."

"You have her name. Surely that's a start." Lack of sleep and ghosts talking in my head had ruined my normal chirpy mood. I couldn't eat. Instead, I cradled the largest mug of coffee I could muster. Enforced socialising with an ungrateful officer-of-the-law was at the bottom of my To-do list. Talking to the recently deceased was a whole new level of weirdness, and I needed some alone time to compute what had happened.

"The name of the boat would help. Are you both sure she didn't remember?" Dave stirred sugar into his coffee. *Sugar! No one who respects the java bean adds sugar!* I was so happy to have moved on from the ridiculous crush I had on him when we first met. My sister was welcome to him and his coffee adulterating ways.

"Dave, darling. The poor girl had a traumatic experience, bless her. I wish I could help you more. But she had to go. There was nothing else she could tell us. I felt, though, that she recognised the name." Cindy was so serene, so matter of fact about what had just happened. I doubted I would ever accept this mumbo-jumbo calmly. "Did you pick up on that, Jess?"

"There were two names. And yes. I think it was familiar to her somehow." *Listen to me! I need to get away!* I took this marker in the conversation to make good my escape. "If I think of anything else, I will tell you straight away, but I have to get to work. Lots to do to prepare for the wedding of the century on Saturday. I don't have the time to sit around. I will pray for her loved ones in my study. I'm sure Mum will look after you all."

Settled behind my mahogany desk, I put in a call to the Boss. Prayer has always been my greatest comfort. In the past six months, I had sought its refuge more and more. Returning to Wesberrey and learning about my pagan roots had challenged my faith. Discovering I had these mystical powers, derived from generation upon generation of family goddess protectors, challenged my sanity. Now, it seemed, I could talk to the dead! This latest development would take some time to process. If I were alive in the seventeenth century, I would burn myself at the stake.

I had half-accepted I could sense stuff, feel events, relive the trauma, and so on. But to hear Ellen Findlay's thoughts in my mind as clearly as if they were my own? That was a whole new level.

The past six months had brought so much change. I felt a little overwhelmed by it all. Now wasn't the time to lose the plot, though. My parish secretary, Barbara Graham, was soon to become Mrs Phil Vickers. The big day was on Midsummer's Eve, and the countdown had begun. The parish was pulling out all the stops to give its favourite couple a wonderful day. As the central coordinator for their impending nuptials, my diary for the week was fit to bursting. The last thing I needed was to get involved in another mysterious death.

# Norma Jean Baker

The sun blazed through leafy boughs as I made my way down to the Cliff Railway. I could have taken Cilla, my wonderful orange scooter, but that would mean stuffing my head into a tight helmet and, as it was such a glorious day, I wanted to feel the gentle breeze through my hair. It also provided the perfect excuse to touch base with my churchwardens, Tom and Ernest, who I knew would be volunteering on the morning shift.

"Our suits arrived yesterday! Ernest looks so handsome in his. Trims the tummy area down, a well-fitted waistcoat, don't you find, Reverend?"

"I guess it does, Tom. One blessing as a vicar is that chasubles are very flattering. I was planning on wearing the white Holy Spirit one, from my Welcome Service."

"Excellent choice. Have you seen the bride's gown yet? Barbara is keeping it very close to her chest." Tom punched my ticket and handed it to me as I stepped across the metal threshold, pulling the funicular railway's burgundy and gold cabin doors closed behind me.

"No, it's the best kept secret in town. My sister, Zuzu, has been helping her with the fittings. Apparently, they think little of my sense of fashion and have not sought my opinion."

Tom cast his expert sartorial eye over my black blouse and cardigan combo and nodded in agreement. "Wise decision, no offence, Reverend." He pressed a button. Metal churned, and the cabin started on its creaky descent to the other station on Harbour Parade. The view of the bay was spectacular. The early morning sun glinted on the blue water. The air was so clear I could see to Oysterhaven and the countryside beyond. On the distant horizon, I could make out the medieval spire of Stourchester Cathedral.

My thoughts turned to poor Ellen Findlay. She couldn't have been thirty years old, if that. It was hard to tell from what remained of her body, but her voice was young. Such a tragedy. What had happened on board that ship? Boat? Yacht? We had little to go on except her name. The most frustrating thing about this 'gift' is that one never gets all the answers, only fragments. Ellen couldn't tell me what she didn't know. Was her death the result of an accident? She didn't sound drunk. But do ghosts stay drunk? Landing in the cold water must have sobered her up. So would dying, I should think. *Jess, listen to yourself! You sound stark staring crazy!* The thud of the car arriving at the harbour platform bumped me back to reality.

"Good morning, Reverend Ward. It's a truly fine summer's day, isn't it? And the forecast is for more of the same for the next fortnight. Bodes well for the upcoming nuptials," Ernest greeted me with an uncharacteristic sunny disposition. His general mood had been less serious of late. Probably this was due to probate finally being granted on Lord Somerstone's estate and the last arrangements of the will settled. "I understand your sister, Rosie, is opening her new shop at the end of the month. I'm sure it will be very successful. She has a good head for business, that young lady."

"Yes, she has." I replied, "There has been so much to sort out, what with the move into the cottage and everything. Thankfully, she is taking a lot of Mum's furniture with her. You wouldn't believe how crowded the vicarage is right now."

"I expect you will be happy to get the house back to yourself again, though I dare say you will miss having your mother's home-cooked meals." Ernest was right. I craved peace and solitude, but the thought of having to fend for myself again was an unwelcome prospect. I was sure the vicarage would remain the main family gathering place, but the days of coming back from work to a warm plate of delicious food and a clean house were numbered. Rosie and Luke moved into the cottage on Love Lane last week. Zuzu and the Baron were renting an apartment in the trendy, and expensive, marina overlooking Stone Quay, and soon Mum would be gone too. It would be just me and the cat - Hugo. I was convinced he would rather be with anyone else.

Hugo and I had an understanding. It was as if he knew I was allergic to his fur and so had established early on that I was a provider of food and shelter, not tummy rubs. For them, he went elsewhere. He had bonded with my sister Zuzu, but her fancy new apartment is a stark white minimalist dream. The black hairball was not welcome, and not primarily because he moults, big time. The apartment was her private sanctuary. A place where she had the Baron all to herself.

In the past, my sister collected hearts like I collect Murano glass fish. Excited at first with the prospect of a new find, only to leave it to gather dust on the sideboard before moving onto the next one. Inspector Lovington was different. With him, she was a predatory, obsessed, full-on bunny-boiler. It wasn't just his money, or that he was the fourth son of a baronet, a dashing police officer, or ridiculously handsome. This was *la grande passion*! Words like love and lust failed to touch the sides. Their relationship was hotter than the Carolina Reaper pepper. I was happy for her, but to be honest, being around them was... well, nauseating.

I had tried convincing Rosie to take Hugo with her, but as she rightly pointed out, she was starting her new business, 'Dungeons and Vegans', and didn't have time to look after another living creature. Fortunately, Luke was old enough to fend for himself. Not that he was at home much these days; now he too had found love with Tilly.

The last escape route for my feline friend rested with Mum. She was very fond of the fluffy demon. Hugo loved her culinary skills. I would miss him, though, if he went.

The unexpected early start meant that I was in town before the tourists poured out of the various temporary B&B rooms the local residents offered for the Regatta at this time of year. The Cat and Fiddle pub was full, as were the small hotels along the coast on the mainland. The Wesberrey Regatta drew pleasure boats and racing yachts from all over the world. The death of one of these visitors would throw a cloud over the rest of the week.

Wesberrey's small harbour, reaching from the ferry landing along the front of Market Square and past the marina and industrial concrete seawalls of Stone Quay, lay packed with vessels of all shapes and sizes. Nautical bunting flapped at the seagulls gliding on the breeze. They hovered aloft, awaiting their opportunity to swoop below and snatch a discarded morsel of fish. Not that there would be many morsels left after the resident feral cat colony staked their claim.

Poor creatures. The dense carpet of boats beneath them should spell rich pickings, except these were not fishing vessels moored with their catch after a long night on the open sea. These boats traded in champagne and canapes.

I strolled along the front to the ferry port. Bob McGuire was resting on a stripy deckchair in between runs to the mainland. Bob knew everything about the comings and goings in the harbour.

"Hi there, Bob. Gorgeous day, isn't it? I bet you're busy this week." I took off my cardigan and lay it down on the stone wall beside him. "Do you mind if I join you?"

"Looks like you're making yourself at home already, Vicar!"

I placed my rear end on the draped polyester, rested my palms on the wall, and lifted my face to the warm sky. The sun glowed through my closed eyelids. "Did you hear they found a young woman's body washed up on the beach by the lighthouse?" I asked.

"Yup, that I did." Bob leaned down under his chair and produced a tartan flask from a canvas bag. "Tea, Vicar?"

"No, thank you. I hear they think she came from a yacht moored here for the Regatta."

"Probably. Landlubbers with no sense in their heads and no respect for the sea."

"Hmm, yes, but have any of them been reported missing in the last twenty-four hours or so?"

"Nope." Bob poured milky brown liquid into the white plastic cap of the flask and took a sip. "But then it is still early in the day for most of them unless they are racing. Might take a while for someone to notice one of their party isn't in the bed they're supposed to be."

The thought that her friends and family might not have missed Ellen yet was heart-breaking. She had only been in my head for a few minutes, but she felt so alone, so isolated. *Maybe all departed spirits feel like that.* She must have loved ones who, when they find out about her tragic fate, will mourn her loss deeply.

Bob threw the dregs of his drink against the harbour wall and screwed the cap back on his flask. "Are you taking the ferry to the mainland today then, Vicar?"

I shook my head. I wanted to walk around the harbour front, see if I could sense Ellen anywhere. If she was on a yacht, there would be others on board, a crew member at least who might explain what happened to her. I just needed to find what boat she had been on.

I left Bob to his work and settled my mind. I planned to walk up and down the jetties and try to feel Ellen's presence. Six months ago, I would have slapped myself for thinking such nonsense. I had no other leads to follow, and though I doubted it would work, it was all I could think of.

Bob was right. As I passed by the expensive vessels packed along the front, the only people milling about above deck were crew members testing equipment, scrubbing the decks, or preparing brunch. I toyed with the idea of calling out to them to enquire if they had a spare bed on board but decided that was an ambiguous opening question and might not elicit the desired response. Even with my dog collar, I was not immune to suggestive overtones. Instead, I simply asked if they had an Ellen Findlay on their passenger list. It surprised me how many could not answer that question without referring to their duty logs, but then I suppose one charter is much like any other and names and faces blur.

The rising noon sun beat red hot above my head, and I was running out of wooden pathways to explore. By now, most of the charters had taken to the sea. They filled the channel with their rainbow sails. Only a handful of yachts remained nestled at the far end of the dock. I sped up to reach them before they cast off. As I turned onto the last jetty, my phone rang.

"Jessie, is that you?" It was Zuzu.

"Er, yes. It's my phone. You called me."

"No, I mean is that you on the harbour. Turn around and wave!"

I pivoted one-eighty and on the opposite side of the road stood my older sister, yahooing across the bay. The dazzling sun bounced off her blonde crown, giving her a saintly aura. Zuzu breathed out sunshine.

I rushed over to the bench where she had parked herself to watch the flotilla. This part of the marina was a few hundred yards away from the pristine apartment she rented with the Baron. The area could rival the French Riviera for affluence and style. A small enclave of refinement on our eclectic island.

"I didn't expect to see you hanging around on the harbour front. What a pleasant surprise! It's not been the same since you moved out."

"Do you miss me, little Sis?" Zuzu ruffled my hair and tweaked the end of my nose.

"Ow! That hurt!" And it did. "Don't make me regret walking over here. Next time I'll walk away."

"Nah, you can't resist a good gossip. It's a stunning view, isn't it?"

"Yes, all those white sails against the shimmering blue. Beautiful."

"Indeed. All that money! Do you know what's wonderful about today, Jessie? Eh? I am here and all those handsome, rich men are out there, and I have zero desire to court any of them. I mean, think about that for a second. I'm thrilled with what I have. I am... not sure I can even say it, content." She tugged at the sunglasses on the top of her head and slipped them onto the bridge of her nose.

"Well, the Baron is quite the catch. You have a lot of reasons to be happy."

"Oh, he is gorgeous. And intelligent, wealthy, loving and *so* good in bed. I am amazed he has the energy to get up at the crack of stupid to go poking around dead bodies after the workout we have every night. But that's the point, Jessie." Zuzu adjusted her Gucci shades and peered over them. "When he leaves in the middle of the night, I know he's coming back. *And* I want him to. I miss him when he's not around. He invades my every thought. I consider him in every decision."

"And you have never experienced this before?"

"Nope."

We sat in silence for a while, letting this revelation sink in. I loved my sister and had often marvelled at her ability to 'find 'em, fool 'em and forget 'em'. She had many conquests and left a long shadow of broken hearts, but I had never thought about why she didn't commit to anyone. I had been in love a few times. To be honest, they were more infatuations, and those were mostly in my youth before I donned the clerical collar. I had my heart broken by them all, except one young man called Hugo, who I met at drama school. It took years to shake him off. He was cute but stubborn, and borderline obsessed with me. I had named the black feline refugee after him because when we first met, I saw him as another pest I couldn't shake off.

"So," Zuzu was first to break the silence. "How are things with you and the handsome headmaster?"

"Yeah, all is fine." Lawrence had asked me out just before Easter. We had been on a few 'dates'. The Old School House proved too expensive to make our regular meeting place, which limited the opportunities for any privacy. It was still early days and both of us were mindful of how our relationship would be seen by the community we both served. It may appear a tad Jane Austen, but tongues wag.

"Have you tasted his wares yet?" Zuzu nudged my arm.

"I am a Vicar. We don't go around tasting men's 'wares'!" I answered with a girlish giggle that set my older sibling to howl with laughter.

"Well, seems a terrible waste of a man to me." She snorted. "Jessie, you need to loosen up. Let rip a little. What are you doing down here, anyway? Seeking to save the soul of some saucy sailor?"

"Ooh, lovely alliteration. Your old English teacher would be proud."

"Mr Kennedy... ah, well, I could tell you a saucy tale or two about him and his extra-curricular activities with the drama club. When I played Roxie Hart in the Sixth Form production of Chicago-"

I closed her mouth with my index finger. "Let's stop this story right there."

Zuzu pulled back and shrugged. "As you wish. Hmm... I wonder if I can get a black flapper mini dress on Amazon. Next day delivery." She whipped out her phone. "I think Dave would love a bit of Roxie."

I knew the conversation was in danger of being sucked into a rabbit hole of their bedroom antics, so I quickly directed us back to Zuzu's original question.

"I was actually down here to see if I could find a yacht. The body that washed up this morning, I think she fell off one of them. She couldn't remember the name."

"Oh, right, you did that medium stuff with Cindy. Dave mentioned it when he called. That's the other thing, you know. He calls me all the time with lots of mind-numbing information, and I actually want to listen to him. I don't even switch off when he talks about cricket. I mean, that must be love, right?"

"That's what all the poets say." I quipped.

"Ha-ha, very funny. So, we are speaking to dead people now, eh?"

"I guess so." Since returning to the island, my sisters and I had learnt little of the mystical family past we were due to inherit. Mum and her two sisters were miserly with any details. They were always so cryptic. I could never understand if their reticence was because of embarrassment, or fear, or over-protectiveness. When Zuzu and Rosie were living at the Vicarage, we would often spend a late night discussing what all this wizardry actually meant and had even given our mother and aunts a suitable nickname. "The 'Charmed' are slow at giving up their secrets. Very enigmatic, the three of them. They all have some ability or other. They sense stuff. I guess you do too. Remember, we needed you and Rosie to do that energy work before. Maybe it's just a strength in numbers thing. Have you had any weird stuff happen?"

"Not really," Zuzu replied, "but then I haven't been testing it like you have." She relaxed beside me, stretching out her legs across the pavement, and she slipped her cotton skirt up to expose her taut thighs to the afternoon sun. Zuzu was several years older than me, and there was not a hint of cellulite. *It's a good thing I am not a vain creature, or I could easily hate my sister.* She clocked my envious glance. "Might as well get a bit of a tan whilst we're sitting here. You must be dying in that all-black ensemble."

"It is rather hot." I fanned myself. *I could murder an ice cream!* "Maybe we could practice a bit of hocus pocus together. See what happens."

"What? Right now? Here on the marina?" Zuzu waved dramatically in front of her and then grinned like the Cheshire Cat. "Why not, eh? I'm not a big fan of your amateur sleuthing ways, too dangerous if you ask me. But this sounds like a fun lunchtime activity. So, should we hold hands or something?"

"I guess," I replied. "Let's try to focus on the name of the boat the girl was on. Her name was Ellen Findlay."

"Got it! Jessie, just one thing. If a handsome vampire appears in a puff of smoke, you can have him. I'm taken."

"So am I." *I think*. "We can give him to Rosie. Deal?"

"Deal." Zuzu cupped my fingers in hers. We both took a deep breath and waited. "Anything?"

"No, not really. I think I can see a white dress?"

"Can you? That's spooky." Zuzu released my hand and sat up. "Do you remember that Athena poster I used to have on my wall back at home? When we were kids."

"You had a few posters," I replied.

"True, but the one of Marilyn Monroe on the air vent, remember? That's what came into my mind when we joined hands. Probably a coincidence, but when you said white dress..."

"Do you think the yacht is called the Marilyn Monroe?"

"Or," Zuzu puffed herself up and pointed at the mooring in front of us, "she was on the '*Norma Jean*'."

Across the road, in all her white gleaming majesty, sat a glorious catamaran with the name 'Norma Jean' in gold italic lettering across her bow.

I rose to investigate further, but Zuzu grabbed my wrist. "You aren't going anyway near the death ship, little sister. I'm calling the Baron."

# All Aboard

D ave arrived twenty nerve-wracking minutes later, riding pillion on the back of PC Taylor's police motorcycle. Throughout the wait, Zuzu and I maintained surveillance on the *Norma Jean*, ready to alert the coastguard if they attempted to cast off.

Zuzu sidled up to her beau and slipped a hand under his shirt. "There have been no signs of life above deck. Maybe it's a massacre?"

Dave wriggled free, his eye twitching. "Let's not get too excited." I wasn't sure if he was referring to the potential mass murder or my sister's sexual advances. "Thank you, ladies, for keeping watch, but PC Taylor and I can take it from here."

I wanted to get on board, see if I could feel Ellen's presence. "Inspector, I would like to join you. We don't know what has happened and there may be people on the yacht in need of spiritual and emotional comfort." The thoughtful expression he sported told me that his mind hamsters were falling over themselves on their wheel as he computed the pros and cons of agreeing to my request. I thought it was worth striking another blow. "And" I whispered, "You saw what happened this morning at the morgue. I promise to share with you if I get anything useful."

"Fine." He pulled out of his pocket several pairs of disposable gloves and handed some to me. "If you feel the urge to touch anything, put these on first. And be careful where you walk. I don't want you contaminating the scene."

"No, sir, thank you, sir!" I almost saluted him like an eager cadet. Instead, I stuffed the gloves into my trouser pocket.

"I guess I'll just stay here and work on my tan whilst you all run off and play cops and robbers." Zuzu stroked Dave's jaw and blew him a seductive kiss before returning to her seat on the bench. His puppy-dog gaze followed her. I wasn't the only one with a magical gift. My sister had cast her spell, and it had totally enthralled this chief of police.

"Erm, the murder ship?" I coughed.

"Yes, yes, of course. PC Taylor lead the way."

The *Norma Jean* was one of only a handful of boats left in the harbour. PC Taylor boarded first, then the Chief Inspector, who held out his hand to pull me up. Drawing closer to the cockpit, PC Taylor paused and, miming with the universal finger on the lips with his left hand and cupping his ear with the right, silently announced there was some activity inside. Dave pressed his ear to the door and kept me back with an extended arm. I obeyed. The last thing I wanted was to be rushed by an axe murderer. Deciding it was safe to proceed, Dave straightened himself up, adjusted his tie, and knocked on the door.

Inside, a frenzied kerfuffle confirmed there were survivors. *Hopefully not a mass murder then.* Dave knocked again. "Open up! It's the police!"

"Hold your horses! I'm coming." a grumpy male voice answered from within. Dave knocked again. "Alright, alright." A weather-beaten face with a nautical white beard and cap opened the door.

"Good afternoon, Captain?"

"Shipton. Captain Jack Shipton. And you are?"

"I am Chief Inspector Dave Lovington of Stourchester Police, this is PC Taylor, and this is Reverend Jessamy Ward. We have reason to believe that one of your passengers may have gone missing." Dave strode across the threshold, forcing Captain Jack to step aside. "Can you assemble all passengers and crew? I will also need to see your ship's log."

"A please would be out of the question, I suppose." mumbled the captain under his breath. He waved to a younger man in a tight-fitting blue t-shirt and white jeans to gather everyone in the saloon. I imagined that the earlier kerfuffle had been people scurrying to nearby hiding places, as it only took a few minutes to bring the full party back. It was clear from their general demeanour they were anxious, possibly even scared. The women were visibly shaken, and a couple appeared to have been crying.

White cushioned benches rounded the saloon in a u-shape facing away from the galley, across the bow. Everyone took their seats as Dave and PC Taylor stood imposingly in front of the bridge door, ready to begin their questions. I pulled myself up on a white leather-topped bar stool to the side. Not the most lady-like ascent, but it offered me a good vantage point over the scene.

There were two crew members. Captain Jack Shipton, whose name and facial hair had, I fantasised, determined his career path. A salty old sea dog who had crossed the equator in merchant ships for longer than most of us on board had been alive. Efficient police probing identified that he hated being relegated to babysitting 'posh idiots' on fancy catamarans, or as he called them 'condomarans', but the pay was good, and he was more or less his own boss.

Next to the captain sat Archie Baldwin, Jamaican native and veteran of the Miami based cruise liner industry, though he was only in his late twenties. His jeans were so tight I had serious concerns about his future ability to have children. Fertility issues aside, I suspected he would have no trouble keeping the women happy. This unofficial part of his job description was as important it seemed as his cooking and deckhand duties. Archie had a cheeky charm, an electric smile, and spent hours exercising to perfect the rest of his appeal. And he would need to keep fit to entertain the ladies on this passenger list.

Celeste Huntsford, the French CEO of the Aurora Agency, oozed Parisian style. She was the creative mastermind behind the marketing agency that had chartered the *Norma Jean* for the Regatta as a team-building activity for her executive team. Younger than her husband, Steve Huntsford, who was comforting her on the sofa, Celeste, though in her mid-fifties, was a woman in her prime. And she knew it. The younger women gathered to her side faded into her shadow.

Even the ebullient Sweetpea Smythe with her fuchsia pink hair and clashing floral fashion paled next to her manager. Like Celeste, she was creative and had the wacky job title of Head of Divine Inspiration. She answered the inspector's questions with a delicate Yorkshire accent. Hailing originally from Hebden Bridge, she studied art and design at the Glasgow School of Art, because she was a huge Rennie Mackintosh fan, but found she had a flair for business and forged a path into corporate marketing for FTSE 500 companies before finally being headhunted by Celeste to join their team two years ago.

Seated at the end of the sofa was Jenny Brown. Like Sweet-pea, I would place her in her mid-to-late twenties, possibly early thirties. *It's so hard to tell.* But that was where the similarities ended. Jenny, Head of Making Magic, aka Operations, was an impeccably dressed mixed-race woman with incredible posture. She perched on the edge of the seat as if anchored to the bottom of the sea by a steel pole. Her face remained expressionless during the initial interview. Occasionally, she would take a quick breath through her nose to re-inflate and restore her inner balance. With fresh oxygen drawn, her shoulders would relax, and she'd cast her green-eyed gaze around the room, like a cat ready to pounce. She was fascinating to watch.

They all were. Especially the money man, Steve Huntsford. If my sister wasn't so loved up, Steve was exactly the type of man she would target. A ridiculously attractive silver fox, Steve had made his fortune working in North Sea oil. Originally from the Scottish fishing town of Fraserburgh, he spoke of his natural respect for the sea and how heartbroken he was to lose another 'family' member to her cruel embrace.

"We are all like family at Aurora. Ellen était notre petite fille. Elle est notre bébé. My baby girl…" Celeste crumbled onto her husband's shoulder.

Dave pressed ahead. "I understand this is tragic news. I have to ask who first noticed Miss Findlay was missing this morning?"

"That would be me, Inspector." Jenny raised her hand. "I knocked on her cabin on the way to breakfast. When she didn't answer, I tried the door."

Dave looked up from his black notepad. "And you found her bed empty. Why didn't you raise the alarm, Miss…" he flipped back through the pages and stabbed his pencil down on an earlier entry, "Brown?"

"Because?" Jenny looked to the others for backup. "I thought she was already in the saloon or perhaps she had gone for a walk or…"

"Okay. Thank you, Miss Brown. And none of you saw Miss Findlay after you all retired following an early supper and drinks on deck?"

"We went straight to bed. Celeste had a headache."

"Mon amour is correct, Inspector." Celeste smoothed away her tears. "The evening belongs to the young n'est-ce pas."

"Indeed. So, you didn't stay up to watch the fireworks?" They all shook their heads. Dave flipped the notebook shut. "The forensics team will be here shortly. We will need to find you all alternative accommodation whilst they process the scene. PC Taylor, we may need to find a secure hotel in Oysterhaven. All the local ones will be full because of the Regatta." PC Taylor nodded.

"Inspector, might I make a quick call?" Steve wrangled his way out from under his wife and stepped towards the front. "I have a friend who lives on Wesberrey. I think she will have room to spare."

"Oh, really? And whom would that be?"

"Lady Arabella Somerstone. Her late husband Gordon and I were members of the same lodge." Steve pulled on his shirt cuff, exposing a bright golden and blue enamel cufflink bearing the Freemason's emblem of a compass and set square. The inspector narrowed his eyes and acknowledged the magical cufflinks with a nod. Steve pulled back his hand, reached into his trouser pocket to get his phone, and then strolled to the galley to make the call.

Moments later, PC Taylor escorted the assembled passengers and crew onto dry land to await a horse-drawn taxi to take them to Bridewell Manor. As they gathered their immediate belongings, Inspector Lovington reminded them all that *no one* could leave the island.

# Bus Stop

"Did you get anything?" Dave asked.

"Not a thing!" I slid off the barstool like a drunk sea lion. *Lady-like, as always.* "I don't suppose you would let me take a sneaky peak in her cabin?"

Dave caught my arm as I steadied myself. "Jess, that would be a total breach of protocol."

"Would your answer be different if I had masonic cuf-flinks?"

Dave screwed up his moustache-edged mouth. "You are infuriating. That was a practical solution to a..." I called in my best puppy-dog expression. "Okay, you win. Come with me. Gloves on."

I whipped the rubbery blue ball from my pocket. "Gloves on."

I didn't know if gloves would hinder my fledgling abilities. I didn't know how any of this worked. But I knew better than to tamper with evidence *before* the forensic team had processed it. Hard science would stand up in court; the voices in my head would not.

I followed Dave along the gangway. The *Norma Jean* was fitted out with glossy wood panels and gleaming chrome fittings. It was all very luxurious but felt claustrophobic to me. I found it hard to believe that no one heard or saw anything. Everyone and everything lived on top of each other.

"Do you know which cabin was hers?"

"'Bus Stop' I believe." Dave checked in his notebook. "They are all named after Marilyn Monroe movies."

"Wasn't that her last film?"

Dave paused. "No, that was 'Something's Gotta Give'. She didn't finish it. So technically her last film would be 'The Misfits'."

"Ah, okay. You are a walking Wikipedia."

"No, just a huge Marilyn Monroe fan." *Well, that explains why you are attracted to my sister.* "Here we are."

The inside of Ellen's cabin had little to tell us on the surface. Her bedsheets were as smooth and tight as a Hollywood facelift. Was that a clue to her ability to make hospital corners? Or had Archie done that as part of his more domestic chores? There was scant evidence that she had stayed there at all. Her clothes were still in her suitcase on a stand. She either didn't have the time or inclination to hang them up or transfer them to the drawers provided. When I am staying somewhere, I live out of my suitcase, so I couldn't judge her for that. However, someone so cavalier about hanging up their dresses is unlikely to give so much attention to their folded sheets. There was an open silver laptop charging on the desk. Toiletries and makeup sat snugly in a cosmetics bag in the ensuite bathroom. And a dog-eared copy of Dale Carnegie's *How to Win Friends and Influence People* lay on a shelf beside the bed. It was a well-thumbed volume, with mini post-its and pencil markings. It was the only really personal item in the room. Not much to show us who Ellen was or why she died.

"Try not to disturb anything." Dave stood back in the doorway to give me some room.

"I'm not sure how this all works. It's all very new to me."

"I know, Cindy explained. I'll admit I'm having a hard time wrapping my head around it all, but your aunt has a gift and I respect her a lot."

"Yup, that's about where I am with it all, too. Can I try the laptop?" I moved the mouse pad with my gloved finger. A message appeared on the screen. "Darn, it's locked."

"Maybe you can work out the password? Is she still in your head?"

"I don't think so. Not like she was in the hospital. Can I sit down?" Dave agreed, and I pulled out the chair in front of the desk, sat down, and closed my eyes. "It's numeric. No, letters, then numbers. Like... like someone's initials and date of birth."

The heat of Dave's body told me he had moved closer. "Are they her initials? E.F.? Might be her D.O.B. People really shouldn't do that."

"No, not hers. I don't think so... It's not family either. Someone she admires, maybe? I just can't see any more."

"You are doing great. Cindy said you have to have faith."

"Did she now." *I have faith, just not in any of this.* "Maybe you should call her in. I feel tired. I don't think any of this helps."

"It does. I can get the tech guys to work out the password. Maybe you are closer to the answer than you think."

I pushed back the chair and worked my way around the rest of the room. "There is nothing else. Don't you think it looks like she didn't sleep here? I mean at all."

"Well, they boarded two days ago, so presumably she spent at least one night here."

"Unless she slept somewhere else? Perhaps she died on the first night and they are all covering it up? Or Archie provides an excellent turndown service."

Dave grinned "I think Archie prides himself on his excellent turndown service." We both giggled. "You have a wicked sense of humour for a woman of the cloth, Reverend Ward. Shall we take a quick tour of the yacht before the forensics team gets here?"

"Lead the way, Inspector."

*****

My gift gave me no further insights. Dave received a call to warn him that the forensics team had arrived on the ferry, and I made my escape to Zuzu's apartment. This was a police matter, and I had done all I felt able to do to help. The yacht party had decamped to Bridewell Manor, and there were no more images or voices in my head.

Zuzu has a stunning new Gaggia coffee machine and the smell of freshly roasted Columbian, and the comforting sound of spurting boiling water was all I could focus on.

"Here, you've earned this. Let's drink on the balcony." Zuzu wedged herself in the open gap and pushed back the sliding glass door with her bottom, two steaming cups of coffee in her hands.

The view from their apartment was glorious. I wanted to let the afternoon sun ease my troubled spirit, but my mind wouldn't rest. Ellen's voice was like a distinct echo disappearing in the caverns of time. I tried to pick her out, but with every minute she grew fainter and fainter. I wasn't sure it was even her voice anymore. I often use my date of birth as my password, perhaps I guessed that detail. Maybe it wasn't a message from Ellen at all. Was I imposing my thoughts onto hers - if hers were ever really there? I was so sure this morning, but now?

"Well, you got her name right." Zuzu was enjoying this. "And we both worked out the *Norma Jean* connection. Jessie, explain that if it wasn't because we are gifted, eh? You can't. You can't deny any of it."

"The Baron is very accepting of all this mumbo-jumbo; I mean for a police officer."

"Yes, strange that. He is wonderfully enigmatic sometimes. He never mentioned his Marilyn fetish. I can work wonders with that."

"I really don't want to know, Sis. Okay? Let's change the subject. Barbara's wedding dress. What can you tell me?"

"We're all booked into Scissor Sisters for a complete makeover on Friday. Put that in your diary right away." Zuzu pointed directions at my phone. "Barbara didn't want a hen party, so we are all going to gather at the hairdressers and ambush her." *This is the first time I'm hearing about this plan!* "Don't worry. Jessie! It's all going to be very genteel and dignified. Rosie's doing some snacks and stuff. Then the twins will style her on the big day. I can't tell you much about the dress except that it's lacy and off-white and she's bought some amazing earrings off Etsy. Custom-made. She is going to look beautiful."

"I'm sure she is. And catering for the reception?"

"Rosie is all over that, too. We can't have Phil cooking for his own wedding."

"No, of course not. Well, I know Barbara arranged the flowers. I spoke to the florist yesterday. She'll be in the church first thing Saturday morning. And the leaflets for the service arrived yesterday. Rosemary has been practising the wedding march and Lawrence has tamed the melodicas. The school choir was in fine voice last week. If the weather is like this, it will be perfect."

I took a sip from my cup and offered a brief prayer for the happy couple.

*No more dead bodies, please.*

# Eggy Soldiers

"How did your Monday go?" Sam reached over to refill my glass with a fruity chardonnay.

"Much the same as usual. If you take out the talking to dead people part." I folded my legs up onto the couch and positioned my rear tight into the corner to get the best possible position for a lengthy gossip.

"Well, I am honoured you invited me over after the day you have had. You must be knackered after that early start."

"Well, you were up too." I pointed out. "I just wanted to see what you thought of it all. I'm not sure I know what to make of it."

"Which bit? Dishy Dave being so unscientific about everything or you turning into the kid from the Sixth Sense?" Sam pulled up a cushion over her face, lowered it to her nose, and hissed, "I see dead people."

"Haha, very funny." I grabbed the cushion and threw it across the room. "Dave is a complex creature. Zuzu is besotted." I sighed.

"You sound jealous, which is just plain greedy, if you ask me. You have a handsome admirer in Lawrence."

"I do. He is really sweet. I declare my heart skips a beat when I hear his name." *Why have I come over all Southern Belle?*

"Why Miss Ward, I do believe you're blushing!" Sam grinned over the top of her glass. She raised a flamboyant hand to her forehead, faking a swoon. "Lawrence! Lawrence! Lawrence and Jessie sitting in a tree, K.I.S.S.-"

"I.N.G. yeah, yeah, yeah." I waved the conversation on with my free hand. "At least another death means you'll get some booty time with Leo Peasbody."

Sam's grin caved. "No, I won't. The coroner took Ellen Findlay away this afternoon."

"Look, I know it's none of my business, but I'm sure Leo would want more of a proper relationship. I know you do, despite all this bravado."

"He has his family and the business."

"Sam, his sons are full-grown men. Why don't you call him - we could all go on a double date?"

My best friend traced her finger along the rim of her glass. I reached across and patted her foot. Not the greatest show of affection, but it was the nearest part of her to me at that moment.

"What's up? I think the two Ls will get on. And we've done nothing nice together since I moved here. It'll be fun. No pressure."

"The two Ls?" Sam rubbed her eyes. It was late, and she had been up even earlier than me.

"Leo and Lawrence."

"Ah, yes. Sorry. I must be more tired than I thought. I blame the wine."

"Hey, why don't you kip here for the night? Mum went to bed hours ago. You have your choice of bedrooms. I recommend Rosie's old room. It's quaint if you like chintz."

"Would you mind?"

"Not at all."

"Well, in that case, let's have another glass."

*****

Tuesday morning shone through the kitchen window. *Is it acceptable to wear sunglasses for breakfast?* Earplugs would be good too. Mum was in full Snow White mode.

"Sam's just taking a shower." she beamed. "Looks like you both had a long night. Coffee?"

I cracked one eye open. "Make mine a double." *I think I've eaten Hugo's cat litter.*

Talk of the black devil. My squinty eye caught the end of his tail escaping through the cat flap. Probably off to see his girlfriend, a sleek white kitten with tortoiseshell highlights Luke had named Paloma.

"Mum, d'ya think we will come home one day to a cupboard full of fluffy mini Hugos?"

Mum put out a coaster for my coffee and sat opposite me. "No, they're just good friends. I think he's too old for that type of shenanigans."

*I know how he feels.*

"It's nice to have company for breakfast. The house has been quiet of late."

"Mum, you had Cindy and Dave here yesterday. It's not too late, you know, to change your mind. You don't need to buy the cottage. Stay here. There's plenty of room."

"We both need our space. You'll just miss having me acting as housekeeper."

This was true, but I would miss her company more. And her potential new home, whilst extremely picturesque, was on a remote part of the island. "Just think, you could use all that money to travel the world first-class if you wanted."

"I could. Ah, Sam, perfect timing; I'll take your eggs out of the pan."

Sam was too squirrel-tailed for a morning after the night before.

"How do you do it? Why don't you have a marching band in your head?"

"Years of training." Sam stretched across the table to grab a slice of toast. "Thanks, Mrs Ward. It's just like the old days. Remember how I was always around yours for supper after school?"

"I do indeed. What was the name of your other friend?"

"Karen Clark." Sam and I answered in unison.

"Lovely girl. Any idea where she is now?" Mum asked as she placed two steaming boiled eggs in front of us.

"No, we lost touch. Her mother passed away, lung cancer, and Karen went to stay with her uncle or something." Sam crunched down on her heavily buttered toast. Her skinny frame could cope with that level of calorific deliciousness. *Why am I surrounded by thin people?*

"Perhaps we should try to find her. Get the Wesberrey Angels back together." Eggy soldiers, delicious part-boiled eggs - still housed in their warm shells - guarded by strips of toasted bread. The perfect start to the day. I sliced open the top of my prey. The golden yolk oozed over the sides. I dragged my finger up the small porcelain cup to catch the drips.

"Jessamy Ward, how old are you?"

"Right now, Mum, I feel like I'm ten again. And it's wonderful."

# Moving On

A couple of paracetamols later and my headache was in retreat. I had promised Barbara that I would swing by the Cat and Fiddle in the morning to talk through the last-minute arrangements for Saturday. Barbara had offered to come to the vicarage, but I thought it would be best to not confuse the roles of parish secretary and bride-to-be. I had given her and Phil the week off to prepare and a further two weeks off afterwards for the honeymoon. They were going to Venice. Barbara had always wanted to be serenaded on a romantic gondola ride through the canals.

"To think this will soon be my new home! Change is in the air and no mistake, eh, Reverend? We all seem to be moving house, moving on."

"Have you decided what you are doing with your cottage?" Barbara grew up on Wesberrey and still lived in her parents' old house, though they had died years ago. This was a momentous life change for her, and I detected she was nervous.

"I am thinking of renting it out. Can't let... I'm not ready to part with it. Anyway, what if this doesn't work out, eh? Don't want to put all my eggs in one basket."

"You and Phil will waltz into old age together, my friend. You are meant for each other."

"Ah, that we are, Vicar!" Phil's cockney tones boomed over from behind the bar. "This Saturday, I'm going to be the luckiest man in the 'ole world. Who knows, maybe we'll ditch the pub and I'll start growing prize-winning marrows and radishes."

"Not married to me you won't, Phil Vickers. I hate marrows and radishes!" Barbara's rosy cheeks spread crimson across her face and neck. "He knows that, too," she whispered. "Reverend, are we doing the right thing? Getting married, that is. I've been alone for so long. I'm not sure I will…"

"Live happily ever after?" Like every bride there ever was, Barbara was getting cold feet. "All I know is that I have married many couples and none of them had the bond that you and Phil have. You are the yin to his yang. The Bonnie to his Clyde."

"Well, that didn't end too well, did it?" she laughed.

"Er, no. You are the Barbara to his Phil, then. Just destined to be together."

Out of the corner of my eye, I could see her fiancé approaching with a tray laden with mid-morning beverages and homemade cake. *The wedding cake! Who was making the cake?*

Rosie was in charge of the catering, but I had heard no mention of the cake. As soon as I left the Cat and Fiddle, I tried to get my baby sister on her mobile, but it just kept going to voicemail. *She's probably at the shop.* I set off across the square.

My family had inherited the old book shop following a bizarre series of events and Rosie, in need of a business opportunity, stepped up to take it on. Whilst she had been drawing up plans for months, she couldn't officially gain access until they granted probate, and now she spent every waking hour and then some getting everything ready for the launch at the end of June.

I had been so busy I had hardly set foot inside the premises since Ernest handed my sister the keys. Even from across the road, it was clear she and Luke had been hard at work. The place was unrecognisable.

Where Island Books had been a brown dusty carbuncle darkening the corner of Market Square, Dungeons and Vegans stood bright orange and proud. All the exterior woodwork shone like a giant satsuma in the mid-morning sun. The windowsills smiled pink lipstick smears of potted geraniums. On the pavement, ornate cast iron furniture sat primed with a grey undercoat ready for their next layer. Rosie was curled underneath a table, brush in hand.

"Wow, little sister, you have been busy!"

Rosie shuffled out and pushed back a few stray auburn hairs with the back of her brush hand. "Do you like it? A bold choice, Pumpkin Latte, but it should get people's attention."

"Is that the name of the colour? Perfect choice. I can't wait till you open. Sorry, I haven't been much help."

My sister rose and pulled out a grey chair. "Here, take a seat. It's dry." She balanced her brush on the paint pot and rested her behind on a table. "Honestly, we've been fine. Tilly and Buck have been helping. And Mum. Even Zuzu moved a stack of old magazines the other day." *Now I feel even more guilty.*

"Good to hear everyone is rallying round. Buck too. He's quite the character, don't you think?"

"He's a good man." Rosie became suddenly very occupied with the button on her dungarees.

"He is." *Now.* A reformed soul. Proof that everyone can change. "Perhaps we should invite him for dinner at the vicarage to say thank you?" *Matchmaker, matchmaker, make me a match.*

61

"Er, yes. That would be... nice." She smoothed her hands down her denim front. "Do you want a tour while you're here? See what we've been up to?"

Rosie skipped over the threshold and, dodging piles of books, led me through to the gaming salon at the back of the shop. Luke was busy with a bunch of coloured wires on the floor.

"Hey, Aunt Jess. What d'ya think? This will be sweet when I'm finished."

"I'll have to take your word for it," I replied. "Haven't you got exams?"

"All done. Aced the lot, naturally. Perfect timing, eh? Means I can concentrate on my den." In total contrast to the bright exterior, the 'den' was virtually pitch black. Though there were several neon signs dotted around the walls and a few action hero posters, they did little to lighten the aesthetic. In the centre stood a large black ash table with various cubby holes underneath.

Luke bounced up with such speed his dark curls took a few seconds to catch up. "Buck made it. It's totally awesome. There's storage underneath for cards and figures. And over here," He danced over to a red metal locker in the corner, "we can store maps and stuff. And look, see, the table even has pull-out cup holders and a snack tray."

"Customers can play for hours and hours without having to get up to eat. We will bring refreshments direct to their chair." Rosie hugged her son with pride. "Luke has worked so hard pulling all this together. It's completely his concept."

"So, Dungeons at the back and Vegans at the front. I like it."

"It's a bit of a risk on the island. Would be a better business proposition on the mainland, but maybe it's the beginning of a national franchise." Rosie already had expansion plans.

"I don't see why not," I replied. "People need to socialise. Even gamers."

"And vegans. It's the way forward. Mum's come up with a fantastic menu. All super easy recipes, even I can handle, with good margins."

"It's a shame she doesn't want to work here. She might change her mind when everything settles down. I can't see her knitting by the fireside, can you?"

"No, but I can understand why she doesn't want to commit. This is hard work, and she deserves a break." Luke had wriggled free from his mother's clutches and was back to the plastic-coated spaghetti on the floor. Rosie's free arm linked through mine, and we walked back outside. "By the way, I was thinking. Hugo can come and live with me if he wants. What's a bookshop without a cat, eh?"

I felt a sudden urge to cry. "We'll have to ask him. He's very picky." I croaked.

# Brief Encounter

Rosie flatly refused my offer to stay and help with the painting. *I could get a complex.* I headed instead towards the Norma Jean. Forensics were probably finished by now, and without the Inspector's presence, I might get something a second time around.

The yacht remained cordoned off with flickering blue and white ribbons. Not much of a deterrent to the determined trespasser. As I drew closer, I spied two familiar characters sitting on the bench Zuzu and I had sat on the day before.

"Captain Jack, are you not allowed back on board yet?"

"No, Vicar. They're taking their own sweet time, and that's a fact. I've got a question for you too, as you're here."

"Of course. May I sit down?" Jack and Archie budged up to give me room. "Thank you, how can I help?"

"Well, to be honest with ya, I thought it odd, the Inspector bringing you onboard yesterday. Offering solace to the bereaved, etc. You know, seemed a bit premature, but folk on Wesberrey be stranger than most. Given that we apprised you of the facts as they stand, I was thinking... do you think a boat can be cursed?"

"I don't think so, no. Bad things happen, often to good people, all the time. Curses offer the superstitious a way to explain things we want to find answers for when there aren't any obvious explanations."

Archie became jittery. "Old man, you never told me about no damn curse!"

"There wasn't one. But now there's been a death. A bad omen at sea. Bad enough having women on board, but that's business. I'm thinking of selling her. Maybe it's time for me to drop anchor for good."

"Jack," his eyes bore into me, "I mean, Captain, this is an extremely upsetting thing to happen, but we don't know yet what caused it. It might have been a tragic accident."

"And that is better for a ship, how? I am rigorous in my adherence to health and safety."

"I second that." Archie folded his muscular arms across his well-defined chest. *Do men deliberately buy their t-shirts two sizes too small to achieve this effect?* "The Capt'n here is a stickler for the rules."

"I take it those rules don't stretch to fraternising with the guests?"

Archie unfolded his arms and rubbed his palms up and down on his thighs. "I am all about the hospitality." He grinned, "Always pays to be friendly. If you know what I mean."

Archie had a face and a body designed to keep the customers happy. I suppose there is nothing wrong with hiring some eye candy to keep the paying guests entertained. What he will do for tips was not my place to judge. "So, I guess it's your job to get to know your customers extremely well?"

"I think it's my greatest skill, Reverend. Some just want to talk and that's fine with me. I love to listen. Others have more, let's say, energetic plans, but hey, I can accommodate that too." His smile was like an electric bulb. Once lit, its brightness was dazzling. It was easy to see the appeal. "Most just want to feel special. It's a fantasy. Like Disneyland. My job is to keep them satisfied. Excellent food, good company. What's more important in life?"

"And the ladies on the *Norma Jean*? How well did you get to know them?"

"What makes you think it was just the ladies?" he chuckled. "But yes, I have some insights."

"Well, I have none that would be of any value," piped in the captain. "I keep myself to myself. Two nights ago, I hit the Cat and Fiddle for last orders as soon as we docked. Left them to watch the fireworks - loud, whizzy things. What the passengers got up to after I left is none of my concern."

"So that was Sunday night, and the landlord of the pub should be able to verify your alibi?" *One less potential suspect. I would need to check with Phil...*

"Not that I need an alibi, Vicar. All of this has nothing to do with me!"

"No, no, of course. I was just thinking that will make the police's job easier." Captain Jack was a mighty curmudgeon, but then it would be natural for an innocent man to be reviled by the thought he might be a suspect.

"Archie, I think you'd better guard your words, my son, before the coppers fit you up with this nonsense. I don't trust that Inspector as far as I could throw him. That poncy moustache. Grow a real beard man!"

I suppressed a giggle to defend my sister's lover. "Inspector Lovington is an honourable man. I am sure he seeks the truth. There will be no stitch-up."

"Easy for you to say, Vicar. Not a young black man, are you?" Jack leaned across his colleague. "I've worked with Archie here for the past three years and never had a better first mate. Straight as a dye."

The Captain's ideas of morality were questionable. I suppose Archie was straightforward in his extra-curricular dealings. His honesty was refreshing.

Archie glowed in the light of his captain's praise. "All I know is they were all on edge this year."

"This year? You have sailed with the Aurora Agency before?"

"Yes, Ma'am. They've chartered the *Norma Jean* twice a year for as long as I have been on board."

"Twice a year?"

Captain Jack pumped himself up. "We're booked for the Wesberry Regatta and a late summer tour of the Med every year. Company perks, eh? All expenses paid mini cruises. There was talk of a Norwegian trip to see the Northern Lights, but I guess that won't happen now. Mr Huntsford loves to sail. I give him a turn at the helm on a calm day. I think he likes the solitude of the flybridge. His wife, Celeste, and the other ladies can be... demanding."

"Ya man, you can say that again!" Archie threw his head back.

Jack motioned to Archie it was time to move on. "Doesn't look like they are going to let us back on her today. The sun is high over the yardarm. If you don't mind us, Vicar."

"No, of course not. It's been lovely to chat."

"If you say so, Vicar."

As Jack and Archie strolled back to the pub, I noticed the captain had a pronounced limp. *Surely he hasn't got a wooden leg? Jess, stop that now!* What an interesting duo. I was certain Archie knows more than he is letting on. I needed to prise him away from the captain.

*****

I stayed a while to process what information this chance conversation had unearthed. I needed to find a way to talk to the other people on board the *Norma Jean*, but the inspector had them sequestered up at Bridewell Manor. *Arabella! I would say she owes me a favour, or two...*

I pulled out my phone. "Lady Arabella? Reverend Ward here. I have been meaning to pop over on a social visit for a while. I don't suppose you have any plans for this evening?... oh, of course, silly me, I forgot you are hosting the yacht party. Very noble of you... Dinner, tonight? At eight? I would be honoured... yes, you are right, perhaps I can offer a little comfort in this desperate hour... informal dress? Of course... no need to send Ralph, I can walk up."

As I slipped my phone back into my pocket, I noticed that there was movement on the yacht. It looked like the forensics team were packing up.

# Chasing Shadows

When I was certain the last of the white jumpsuits had left, I wandered down to the mooring and strolled up the gangplank. With all the other yachts out to sea enjoying the beautiful sailing conditions in the bay, I was confident no one had seen me.

I had another pair of blue gloves and even though they had completed the forensics; I didn't want to contaminate the scene by accident. But then again, what if the issue last time was the gloves? Perhaps I need to touch things directly to pick up what they had to say? Only one way to find out...

I headed first to Ellen's cabin. The police had removed her laptop, book, suitcase, and make-up bag as evidence. *This is a complete waste of time!* I flopped on the bed. The mattress, these sheets, were the only connection I had to the dead girl *if* she had even slept here. I laid back and closed my eyes.

Nothing. What if I thought about Archie? If he had been sleeping with Ellen, then maybe I could pick up on that energy. At first, there was nothing, until I felt something or someone pressing down on me. There were definite caresses. Soft, feathery touches on my face, through my hair, along my inner thigh. *I won't mention this part of the investigation to Lawrence.* I wanted to relax into the sensation. If I could go a little deeper, perhaps I would see a face. But there was no intimacy here. It was perfunctory, transactional. Ellen was looking for information. Archie had some information *she* wanted.

*Oh my!* I sat up with a start.

"Did you enjoy your nap?" I recognised the voice.

"Dave! You scared me!" The only way to save face was to brazen it out.

"Well, I didn't want to interrupt." He leaned against the cabin door frame and stroked his moustache "Did you learn anything?"

I straightened up my blouse. It had twisted itself in my trouser waistband. "No, nothing, I'm afraid. How did you know I was here?"

"Just a hunch. I knew you wouldn't be able to resist sneaking back on board once the coast was clear."

"You invited me in to help you with this case, remember."

"No, I didn't. Your aunt did. I merely played along."

"I suggest you have another chat with Archie. He knows something. I believe Ellen was using him to get information."

"And why would you think that?"

"Just a hunch."

"Touché."

"Now, if you don't mind, I have to get back and change. I have a dinner invitation up at Bridewell Manor."

"Oh, do you now? Guess there's no point in trying to stop you." Dave stepped forward and placed a hand on my shoulder. "Jess, be careful. The coroner is pretty certain Ellen's death is suspicious. Someone from that yacht is probably responsible. And they are trapped here. Cornered animals are wont to attack if threatened. And your sister will never speak to me again if anything should happen to you."

"It's just dinner. I'll be fine. Wouldn't want you two lovebirds falling out on my account."

\*\*\*\*\*

Before I could start transforming myself into a delectable dinner guest, there were a few work things I needed to catch up on. What with the wedding and everything, I had been sadly neglecting the day job. Even with choosing to walk up to the manor house, I had several hours to kill. Bad choice of words, but murder was on my mind.

There was a nagging something running around in my head, evading every attempt to pin it down. In the cabin, I knew I was reliving a memory. I had experienced this before. It's a strange sensation. Like I am there and also not there at the same time. I am a witness to events from the victim's or killer's perspective. I feel their motivations but have no tacit knowledge. There is no context, only emotion. Given the scenario, I expected to find passion, desire, lust, but what I experienced was cold and calculating. Not that it wasn't enjoyable. To be witness to such intimate physical sensations was embarrassing. Yet, I felt that the pleasure gained was a bonus and not the reason for the encounter. All this head-hopping was making me nauseous. How do women use sex for profit? This mindset goes against everything I stand for. Where is the love?

I needed a shower to wash the experience away, but first I had to talk to Lawrence. I was desperate to hear his voice and let his calm tones heal my troubled spirit.

I was stretching across the desk to reach my phone when the vicarage landline rang. I paused, waiting for Mum to answer it.

"Jess? It's for you!"

"I'm busy, Mum. Can you get their name and number, and I will call them back?"

Mum's muffled voice floated down the corridor. Then there was a knock on the office door. "Jess, I think you need to come straight away." Whatever was on the other end of that phone, it wasn't good news. My feet dragged my anxious heart to the hall table. "Jess, remember your old school friend, Karen Clark?" I nodded. *We had only talked about her yesterday.* Mum passed me the receiver, her hand covering the mouthpiece. "Her name now is Karen Findlay. Ellen was her daughter."

*****

My earlier enthusiasm for an evening of fine dining and sleuthing at the manor ebbed away over a whiskey-laced cup of tea at the kitchen table. Karen was travelling down on the Caledonian Highlander sleeper train overnight and would arrive at London Euston just before eight in the morning. I had offered to meet her at the county coroner's office in Stourchester at eleven. Sam was going to join us. Whilst we both had been keen to contact our old friend, it was hard to see how the circumstances could have been any worse.

"Ellen was her only child," I sobbed "Mum, what am I going to say to her?"

"You will find the words. This is what you do." A rare arm of comfort snaked its way around my back. "I can't imagine the pain of losing your only daughter. There's no word for it, is there? We have widows and orphans, but we don't have a term for people who have lost a child."

"Karen has no one now, she said. Her husband died five years ago, and now this. I'm glad Sam agreed to come with me. It's been so long. What comfort can we give her? We don't know each other anymore."

"No, but you had an incredible bond when you were young. That will come forth to support her in her hour of need. Invite her to stay here. She's a long way from home."

I agreed. They all were a long way from home. Aberdeen is about as far away as you can get from Wesberrey and still be in the British Isles. *Is it me? Has murder followed me to this place?*

Mum pushed back her chair with a screech. "Come on, dry your tears. You need to get ready for dinner up the road!"

"No way! Someone up there killed my friend's daughter! No way, uh-uh."

"Exactly. And though it rips my heart in two to say it, you are the only one who can help get Ellen justice. Have a shower, throw on your glad rags and paste on a smile. You've got this."

# Tommy

I took my phone with me and curled up with it under the duvet. This gift was a curse, and my curiosity killed more than cats. Death stalked my every move. I had been on this island for six months. Six! And the murder rate had blown off the chart. Before I took up my office at St. Bridget's, the most PC Taylor had to deal with was a spate of flowerpot thefts. Now the chief homicide detective had rented an apartment here to be closer to the crime capital of the county.

*Jess, you're talking nonsense. Dave moved here because of Zuzu, not you. Get over yourself! This isn't about you.*

I scrolled Lawrence's number and hit dial. I needed it to be about me, for a few minutes, at least.

Fifteen long minutes later, my heart sang to the tune of his voice crossing the threshold below my window. A few moments more, and Lawrence's lanky frame lay wrapped around me on the bed.

He stroked the hair from my eyes and brushed his lips along my left temple.

"I'm here for you."

I prayed out the words. "Hold me."

And he did.

*****

We arrived at Bridewell Manor a little after eight. Though still fragile, I finally found the energy to get myself ready and had phoned ahead to warn our host that I would be bringing Lawrence with me. Arabella was delighted because that meant an even number of place settings. Hugh Burton was also staying over in the big house.

"We have made up the blue room for you both. You didn't bring any nightwear? I'll have Ralph go fetch you some up from the vicarage. And a swimsuit. If you don't have one, I'm sure there is one of mine you can have." Arabella snapped a finger.

"Arabella, we weren't planning to stay the night."

My protest fell on deaf ears. "Nonsense. How can you relax whilst watching the clock? You can have a late-night swim under the stars. Shame it's not a full moon yet, but it will still be magical."

"I'm sure it will be lovely, but there's no need to trouble Ralph. I can swim another time."

"Or you could swim in the nude." Arabella found the idea highly amusing. "It won't be the first time. That pool could tell a tale or two."

*Sharing a bedroom, naked swimming.* I looked at Lawrence in horror. Usually, I would have no difficulties in clarifying where I stood, but tonight I was struggling with everything.

Like a valiant knight of old, he stepped forward to defend my honour. "Lady Somerstone-Wright, maybe another time. The Reverend has had a trying day. All we seek is excellent food, pleasant conversation. And..." he whispered, "separate rooms."

Arabella sniggered into the back of her hand. "Excuse me, Jess. I do forget you are a priest, especially when you are out of uniform." *Arabella had been at the cooking sherry.* "And, Mr Pixley, sir, *you* are a gentleman. A rare creature these days. As you wish. *All* are welcome here." Right on cue, her butler appeared. "Ralph, we will need another room for Mr Pixley." Stretching her head to assess his full height, she added. "Looks like he'll need a super-king. The Emerald Suite, I think."

"Yes, Ma'am."

"Tell Annie, we will dine in twenty minutes." She linked her arm through mine. "And champagne. My guests all need champagne!"

The thought of alcohol threw my already knotted stomach into a tailspin. "Perhaps I could have an orange juice instead?"

"Oh, Jessie, loosen up. You never let your hair down. Come, Hugh is simply dying to say hello. We are both so grateful for your discretion. You know, *before*. Ralph and Annie too. We all owe you such a debt of honour. Please, *re-lax*."

*Coming here was a huge mistake!*

The drawing room swam in a sea of chatter. Lawrence offered his arm and guided me towards Hugh, propping up the fireplace.

"Reverend Ward, what an absolute joy! When Bella said you were coming tonight, I was beyond delighted. And who is your handsome companion?"

"Hugh Burton, this is Lawrence Pixley. He is the headmaster of the local school."

"Ah, a man of learning. So, you must be the chappie heading up the new Somerstone Academy. You'll get free rein with all that. Bella has zero interest in any of it."

"Hugh, at some point I need to get you to make a call to my aunt. Seems she's a huge fan of *Above Stairs* and your character in particular. She may talk your ear off with her theories. She was furious when she found out you had stayed at the vicarage, and I hadn't told her."

"My pleasure, Reverend. Shall we do it now before the appetisers? Always have time for a fan."

I had promised Aunt Pamela that I would help her meet her hero, but I mostly welcomed the relative normality of the conversation. Being in a room with Ellen's murderer made me uneasy. How was I going to face Karen tomorrow? I had held her dead daughter's hand. Her final thoughts on this earth had been in my head. I needed some air.

It was a warm night and the drawing room doors opened onto the garden. I tried to make my excuses, but I didn't have enough breath to speak. Taking advantage of Hugh's conversation with my aunt, I mimed my exit and left Lawrence to make my apologies and follow behind.

"Are you okay? We can leave if you want to?" Lawrence bowed down to search my eyes for clues.

"No, Mum is right. I need to be here. I owe it to Karen and her daughter."

Lawrence was being incredibly stoic about everything. Who wants to date a psychic vicar who speaks to dead people? It was a conversation I had avoided for weeks. Since we began seeing each other, I had teased him with the idea that my family had a lot of secrets and there were many things I was struggling to come to terms with myself. Tonight, as I sunk into his firm embrace, I had cried it all out. His response had been to draw me closer. And here he was, literally holding me up.

"We will go back in when you are ready. I can ask questions too. I've read every Agatha Christie novel, and love Dorothy L. Sayers. Quite fancy myself as a Lord Peter Wimsey to your Harriet Vane."

"Oh no, I think we are more like Tommy and Tuppence. Christie wins out every time."

"I might have to fight you on that."

The setting sun cast a halo over Lawrence's blond hair, and I felt secure in his shadow. I tiptoed my face to his and sought his lips. My body pulsed in response to his touch.

"Maybe we should have kept the one room?" I joked. *Doing the right thing is so hard sometimes.*

# Mon Chéri

Ralph had set the dining table with fine gilded porcelain tableware and gleaming crystal that caught the dying amber rays of the setting sun. Arabella and Hugh held their respective courts at either end. Lawrence and I faced each other close to Hugh. I had Archie and Steve on either side. Celeste flanked my partner to his left, opposite her husband, and Sweetpea sat on his right. Captain Jack was deep in conversation with Arabella on Celeste's left, and Jenny was opposite him on my side of the table. Low creamy candles nestled in beds of pink roses; minimal decoration enabled maximum conversation. Alcohol was free-flowing, and spirits were high. It was easy to forget that this assembled party was there as a direct consequence of the tragic death of one of their team.

I took a large gulp of juice and counted to ten. "Steve, tell me more about Aurora. How long has the agency been going?"

"We're heading to our silver anniversary this autumn. I'd planned to charter the *Norma Jean* for a tour of the Norwegian fjords, but old Jack here is threatening to throw in his cap. Wouldn't be the same without him."

"Twenty-five years! Impressive. Your current team is very young. I suppose that's the nature of the business. I imagine marketing requires a certain youthful energy."

"It's vital. We were amongst the first to push into twilight marketing before it even became a phrase. Our clients are global players and need a twenty-four-seven worldwide presence. That means long hours, total commitment, and the ability to adapt at speed. Burnout is real. This is a high-pressure industry. We live or die by results. To stay a top-ten company, I need my staff to sell their souls, and Celeste cracks the whip most devilishly." Steve reached across the table, gathered up his wife's right hand, and leant across to kiss it gently.

"Mon chéri." Celeste pulled back and brushed the back of said hand across her lips.

"How long have you been married?" I asked.

"Twenty-five years. It is our silver wedding anniversary on Saturday."

"Wow, so you started Aurora pretty soon after you got wed."

"Pillow talk during our honeymoon, yah might say. Celeste was, is a fireball of ideas. She had the vision. Celeste recognised the power of digital marketing and saw it was the future. She *is* Aurora. These are our children." Steve gestured across the table.

"And children leave home, I suppose."

"Aye, some of our former employees have set up their own agencies, but most tire of the corporate whirl. One even moved into salmon farming. I believe they have supplied our main course. Arabella has an account." Steve raised his emptying glass in Lady Somerstone-Wright's general direction. "Our bonds are strong. Team building is important to sustainable growth. We expect total loyalty and complete devotion. We're a family, and family businesses mean sacrifices for shared reward. Sweetpea, Jenny, Ellen..." His voice cracked as he swigged down more wine.

"I am so sorry about Miss Findlay. This must be hard for all of you."

Steve nodded. "She was our wee bairn. Been with us a little over six months. She was so looking forward to the Regatta. The girls had told her so much about the fun they had on these trips."

*I bet they did.* I threw a sideways look to Archie who was flirting openly with Sweetpea, her flushed cheeks and décolletage mirroring the colour of her hair.

My mind returned to Karen and the long journey ahead of her. She would be about to board the train. I was curious why Aurora continued to return to the Wesberrey Regatta. It was a relatively minor event on the sailing calendar.

"Why Wesberrey? It's a long way from Aberdeen."

"That it is. But it's much more laid back than Cowes. Ye see I *love* sailing." Steve's Scottish accent ramped up as he spoke. The more excited he became, the broader it grew. "Ye can take the lad out of Fraserburgh, but ye cannae take Fraserburgh out of the man. But the rest of the agency has nay interest in the races. This week is business first, boats second." He paused to butter a roll. "Captain Jack and I go way back. There's no better captain in the charter game. His diary fills quickly, so we struck a deal on the Wesberrey gig years ago. Two weeks a year the *Norma Jean* is ours exclusively, the rest of the time he hires her out for top dollar. Celeste helped recruit Archie for him, he's an impressive young man. Makes for a positive return on our investment."

"You have shares in the *Norma Jean*?"

"Aye." *Of course, how stupid of me!* The first dish of seared scallops appeared. The sun's heat was a distant memory. It must be past nine o'clock. I was starving. "And you knew Arabella's late husband?"

"Gordon? Aye, we were masons together. He went to university in Scotland and hung around up there for a while before taking on his father's construction business. Another reason to choose Wesberrey for our annual jaunt. Lord Somerstone used to throw the best parties. Tell ye the truth. We were all gob-smacked when Gordy landed Bella. I suppose ye know she was an enormous star in the nineties."

I grimaced at the thought of those parties. Parties that had caused my family so much harm. But life goes on. "It must be strange staying here so soon after Gordon's death. Such a tragic end."

"Oh, Gordon probably had it coming." Steve stabbed at his plate. "We were associates, but I never really liked the man. Celeste and Arabella, on the other hand, get on like a house on fire. Have to keep the wee woman happy." Steve winked as he threw a whole scallop into his mouth, chewed quickly and swallowed hard.

"Interesting that your executive team is all women, that must be rare - even today."

"Aye, Celeste prefers it that way. Makes me the alpha male, so nay complaints from me about that. Better eat up there, Vicar, looks like they are bringing in the main course."

*****

As the baked salmon landed, Arabella rose. She raised a glass and using a fish knife clinked the side. "Right, everyone! Men, stay where you are. Ladies all move around clockwise." Duly ordered, I found myself on the opposite side of the table at the end next to Hugh, with Lawrence to my left and Archie opposite.

Lawrence squeezed my thigh. "How are you feeling?" *Don't say tingly.*

"I am better, thank you. I saw you talking to Celeste. Anything to report?"

"I'm relieved she moved on. Does that count?" he sniggered. "She's a very passionate woman."

"I know. They are all a little sex mad, aren't they? See, Archie has already turned his attention to Jenny."

Lawrence blanched. "No, about her business! I barely got a word in. How much can one say about sector analysis and proposition benefits? A lot, it seems." *Could you be any cuter?*

"Well, the agency is her baby. Quite literally, I think. Now Sweetpea is free from playing footsie with Archie. See what you can find out from her. And I will talk with the two handsome gentlemen on my right."

"Try not to enjoy yourself too much." The candlelight danced along his cheekbones, leading me down to his pale lips. I wanted to kiss him to prove my devotion. *Devotion!* Steve had used that word to describe the team's bonds. Instinctively, I knew that was important, but how?

There was no time to think it through. Hugh was topping up my juice with champagne. "Bella has given me strict orders to loosen you up, Reverend Ward. I believe we should count Buck's Fizz as part of our five-a-day. What do you say, Archie? Eh?"

Archie temporarily broke off his attentions to Jenny to offer his glass for a refill. "Yeah, man!"

Hugh grinned as Archie pivoted back in his chair. "Oh, to be young and single, eh, Reverend? The headmaster seems like a good man."

"He is."

"How long have you been seeing each other? He has that look."

"What look is that?" I took a small sip of my drink. I didn't want to appear rude.

"There's a hunger in his eyes. It's subtle. Easy to overlook. Men hunger for two things and two things only. Sport and love. See Archie, his eyes are wild for sport. That young lady is a game for him. His prey, if you like. But the head-master sees you as I see Bella. It is a hunger that can never be satisfied. Women rarely understand the difference, but we men know. I see it in him when he looks at you."

"But surely, you have Bella now? Everything worked out in your favour. You have your prize."

"Yes, Gordon is out of the way. God rest his toady soul. Her father as well. But this is not about winning or taking possession. I have made love to that beautiful woman more than any man, yet it will never be enough. It is about *becoming*. Bella has my heart and keeps me tethered to her like a puppy, but I feel no shame. There is nothing that will ever pull me from her. I have no pride. I have no dreams that are not hers to share, no future without her in my life. With her, I become more than I am alone."

I could feel my cheeks blushing. A quick head tilt reassured me that Lawrence was deep in conversation with his brightly coloured neighbour. "It is early days," I coughed in reply.

"For him, it is eternal. Trust me, Reverend. One day he will offer you his hand. Take it and he will never let you go." *Flaming actors, so romantic!*

"So, this is how you get cast as the leading man!" I quipped.

"I know human nature. I know love." Hugh spooned some buttered asparagus onto his plate. "Steve has that look too."

"Really?"

"Oh, yes. You must have picked it up when you spoke to him. Celeste is his world. He would do anything to please her or protect her."

*Anything?*

# Ladies and Gentlemen

T he ladies moved again when the dessert appeared. Lawrence was now to my left, and Captain Jack to my right. Sweetpea took great delight in being at the head of the table. When the bowls of lemon posset had been scraped clean, she insisted on making a toast.

"To our hostess with the mostest, I give you - Lady Ariadne." *Arabella!* "She swooped in and rescued us from incarceration in the dungeon of a Wesberrey jail." Sweetpea swayed. "Ellen fell, we all know that! Silly fool. She should have been sturdier on her feet, you know. No sea legs, ain't that right, Captain?" Celeste tried to pull her protégé back down into her seat. Sweetpea tugged herself free, almost fell back onto her chair, rounded, and steadied herself with one hand on the table. "She was probably sneaking around, as usual, you know. Anyway, what was I saying? Yes, to our host-tess, Lady Abigail Somersault. Cheers!"

A forest of tense arms clinked crystal above pools of fading candlelight. Toast complete, Arabella suggested we should proceed to the terrace whilst they cleared the table for coffee. We all retreated to embrace the call of the midnight air, each grabbing the opportunity to latch back on to our partners. Jenny whisked Archie out to a loveseat under an old oak, and Captain Jack gallantly offered an arm to the wobbly toastmaster.

"What do you think all that was about?" I asked Lawrence.

"Jess, I'm not sure you want to find out any more about Ellen Findlay. From what I gleaned from Miss Sweetpea Smythe, she wasn't a very nice person. And she's right, it was probably an accident."

"The coroner may say otherwise."

"And you need to be there to comfort your old friend if he does."

"Lawrence, no one else has a bad word to say about her."

"Jess, I think you will find no one says anything about her."

Lawrence was right. Sweetpea's toast was tasteless, and she was obviously drunk, but no one had offered their respects for Ellen - the wee bairn of the Aurora family.

*****

Coffee provided a chance to mingle more. Because of the nature of the seating arrangements for dinner, I had hardly spoken to any of the women present, and I felt they held the key. I hung back, stirring the cream in my cup, waiting for the opportunity to chat with Celeste.

"I had a lovely conversation with your husband over dinner. He is so proud of all you have achieved with the agency."

"Mais oui, the agency has been a marvellous success. Aurora is leading the way in global marketing. We are the best in the world." She nibbled off the tiniest corner of the shortbread biscuit in her hand and balanced it on the rim of her saucer. Her trim figure suggested she was extremely careful with what she put in her mouth.

"He talked about Aurora being a family. Ellen's tragic death must be hard for you all."

Celeste bristled and deflected. "There's a draft? Non?"

"Shall we adjourn to the sitting room? The nights can get quite chilly. I believe Ralph was going to set a small fire."

I had never been in the sitting room before. I'm not sure that was the correct name for it, but it was a cosy furnished room with a soft floral settee and matching armchairs around a low table. It was almost like being back in my Aunt Pamela's front room, though the walls had white painted wooden shelves displaying original Ming Dynasty vases, not G-plan furniture and mid-century Royal Worcester plates. The coffee table was a handy space to place our cups down. Celeste wrapped her silk shawl around her bare shoulders and made herself comfortable in the furthest armchair.

I settled myself on the settee. "This is a magnificent house, isn't it? I understand you have visited many times?"

"Oui, Arabella is like a sister to me. She understands my passion, and we worked on her father's account for several years."

"It's a small world, isn't it? Did you know that Ellen's mother was from Wesberrey? She's an old school friend of mine."

"Mon Dieu! I did not know." She shivered. "A small world, indeed." A mist rose in her eyes. She turned her focus on the fire. "Ellen was, how shall I say, she had a complex personality. I loved her ambition. She knew people, she read them so well. It made her an excellent Head of People Power." *They all have such imaginative job titles!* "We have a huge team. All over the world. Different labour laws, different expectations, and she never shied away from a challenge. C'est tellement tragique, n'est pas?"

As a product of the English state school system, my school level French was woefully poor, but I caught the sentiment. Ellen's death was a tragic waste of talent. What I didn't detect was any sense of personal loss. Celeste appeared upset but remained guarded. Maybe she was just a very private person. Someone who needed to maintain control, despite all her talk of passion.

"Did you ever meet Ellen's mother? You all seem very close."

"Non." She shook out an imaginary crease in her green organza dress and shifted slightly, squaring up to the fire. "We do not meet outside socially. I do not care for their lives outside the Agency. It is unimportant."

"And yet, correct me if I am wrong, you are all most intimate. Archie is very open about -"

"Archie is for my girls, an amusement."

"And for you? Such activities lead to jealousy and -"

Celeste slapped her thigh and leapt to her feet. "Reverend, you are so parochial! Yes, that is the right word. I do not sleep with the help! But, even if I did, why can we not share? They are all adults. He is also a superb cook."

She bent and swirled close to the fireplace. So close that my 'parochial' mind was fearful of her dress going up in flames. "Celeste, please, it is dangerous. Your dress?"

In response, she gathered up her skirt in one hand and continued to waltz around the room. "You think me a paradox. How can I dance when I have lost my baby?" *Her baby?* "But we must always dance when we can dance. Work when we can work. And love... For that -" Celeste fell on the seat beside me, breathless. "For that, Reverend Ward is all we can do. Come, come, the party is next door. You have a handsome man waiting for you. When we have handsome men, we should not dance alone."

*****

I did indeed think her a paradox. One minute she was uber-restrained and controlled and the next she is whirling around the room like a dervish. Celeste had corralled all the couples back onto the terrace to dance.

*Poor Lawrence.* I cursed being short as he stooped down to whisper in my ear. "Jess, she is probably on drugs. Aren't all those types snorting cocaine in the bathroom during their lunch breaks?"

"Let's forget about the investigation for now." I stroked his cheek. "Just kiss me."

And he did.

# Madeira, M'Dear?

After a few turns around the terrace, I needed to make a trip to the little girls' room. To my surprise, Captain Jack was stationed in the corridor outside.

"It's Miss Smythe. I think she's unwell."

I knocked on the door.

"Hold your horses! Gawd, surely there's more than one loo in this mansion?" The door cracked open, and I edged myself around to find the fingers of an outstretched arm losing grip of the handle. "Oh, it's you, Vicar. Come in, Chuck." Sweetpea released the door. I slid into the bathroom before it slammed shut. "Wow, that was loud!" Her pink head disappeared back into the toilet basin.

"Are you okay?"

"Stupid question. I'm clutching a U-bend for dear life, what do you think?"

"Yes, sorry. Here, let me help." I pulled a face towel off the shelf above the sink and ran some cold water. "May I?" I took the garbled sound from the bowl as a yes and knelt down beside her. Pulling back her hair, I wiped her face.

Sweetpea twisted around and fell against the wall, sprayed her legs out in front, and blocked my exit. I flushed the toilet and squeezed down beside her.

"Tough night, eh?"

"Did you see her?" Sweetpea waved her hand around. "Left me with ole Jack!"

"Are you talking about Jenny?

"Of course. You'd think with Ellen out of the way... man, I mean, you know? What does she want him for anyway when she has the boss! It's not fair!"

"The boss? What, is Jenny having an affair with Steve?"

"Oh, you are cute, you know." Sweetpea gulped, paused, puffed her mouth and pushed me back into the wall. *I knew I should have sat on the other side!* Then she pulled back and smiled, "False alarm."

"You were saying, Jenny and Steve?"

"No, silly." she hiccuped, "Celeste! They are always having secret meetings, you know."

"But Jenny's all over Archie?"

"And?" *Indeed, how parochial of me.*

"Did Ellen know about their... relationship? Jenny and Celeste," *That could be a potential motive for murder.*

"Not sure, m'dear. I mean, she was constantly up in everyone's business, you know, so I doubt that escaped her beady little eyes." Sweetpea gestured with her hand for me to pass her the face towel.

"I take it you didn't like Ellen much?"

"Look, I know we shouldn't speak ill of the dead, but I'm not going to miss her. She had a way with her, you know? She pissed off lots of my team. My guys are creative, you know. Sensitive. She just saw them as problems to be solved. Resources to be deployed. Expensive resources. She was always bringing in novel ways to check up on them, you know. Setting targets. Cutting the deadwood, she would say. It's my team, you know, my responsibility. I can be ruthless if necessary. This is a tough business, you know." She mangled the towel on her lap, creating a wet patch on her crotch. "But as long as we deliver for the client, who cares, right? That's the bottom line. But not for Miss 'Show me your receipts' Findlay. You'd think it was her money. Like cut us some slack, you know."

"Yes, I guess so."

Sweetpea continued to wring the towel between her fingers. She seemed impervious to the damp material. Her mind was elsewhere. "She made it very difficult... Still, being the bitch from HR isn't a crime, is it? I mean, we're the same age, you know."

"Could she have been blackmailing Celeste or Jenny?"

"Celeste would have just laughed at her. Why would she care? It's not the 1950s, you know."

"No, but would Steve be jealous? He loves his wife very much." I resisted adding, 'you know,' it was a contagious habit.

"He has forgiven her much worse, you know." Sweetpea's plump breast heaved with buried tears.

"It's okay to cry, you know." *Darn it!*

"I wouldn't be crying for her, Vicar, you know. Just the cherry on the cake when I saw Archie..." She stemmed the rest of her words with the towel.

"You saw Archie go into her cabin that night, didn't you?" Matted pink locks swayed in response. "Were you jealous? That would be understandable."

There was a loud knock. "You okay in there?" It was the captain. I'd forgotten he was on sentry duty.

Sweetpea dragged herself to her feet and called out, "Yes, yes. I'm fine." Pausing at the door, she added, "Thank you for your help, Vicar. I think I'll retire to my room. Too much madeira, you know. Don't know what I am saying."

*****

The alcohol was getting to me too. I swayed a little too much as I made my way back to the main party. I could understand how drinking onboard a yacht would be double trouble. Maybe Ellen's death was an accident. I was so busy trying to stay upright that I didn't see Jenny coming towards me.

"Vicar, is Sweetpea alright? I just saw Captain Jack, and he said she has gone to her room."

"Why, yes, she was feeling unwell. One too many cocktails."

"Poor thing, I understand. They are very generous with the alcoholic beverages here. I don't think my glass has been empty all night. Are you returning to the party? I'll walk with you, if I may."

"My pleasure. We haven't talked properly," I replied. "I wonder if there's any coffee left?"

"If not, I'm sure that gorgeous butler will rustle up a pot. How wonderful it must be to have such a vigorous man on hand at your beck and call."

"Well, you seem to have commanded Archie's attention for most of the evening." Adding a steaming cup of coffee was a direct challenge to my already compromised balancing skills. I narrowly avoided knocking over a jardiniere with obligatory oversized aspidistra as we entered the sitting room.

"Yes, well, he's a company perk." *That's one way to look at it.* "He's gone to check on Sweetpea." *Well, that should make her feel better.*

"I must say, you are all very casual about sharing the company perks. It's an eye-opener for me."

"I suppose it is unusual. Maybe it's because Celeste is French. You know, l'amour, la grande passion and all that jazz."

"Still, it is unusual. It must cause jealousy. That kind of rivalry cannot be conducive to building good working relationships."

"I guess if anyone was to get romantically involved. Which none of us are." I marvelled at Jenny's ability to remain poised and perfectly coiffed, despite drinking all night. I could barely maintain my balance on the armchair. She had landed on the sofa, and despite the sumptuous temptation of its cushions, Jenny was very much in control. There was a lightness to her, like a sparrow buffeted by the wind, maintaining its hold of the branch yet ready to fly again at a moment's notice. Her eyes were cat-like. Maybe feline was a better description. She was elegant, but wary. I felt she was biding her time, waiting for advantageous opportunities to pounce.

"Are you certain none of you wanted more? Sweetpea, perhaps? Or Ellen?"

"Why, was Sweetpea crying over amorous Archie? Don't you go falling for that little act, Vicar. Sweetpea wants to win, just as much as any of us."

"Is Archie a trophy to be fought over?" I was uncomfortable with where the conversation was heading. Whilst the first mate appeared to be enjoying his role as a lothario, I found the situation distasteful and was trying to be open-minded. But was this really all a game?

Jenny's mask broke just enough to leak a patronising snigger. "Archie is irrelevant. He is entertainment, nothing more. He is here to keep us primed. If we can control our sexual urges, channel them into an appropriate vessel, then we can focus our energies on the major prize. The success of the business."

I was shocked. *Give me parochial any day.* What was wrong with these people? Did Ellen pose a threat to their business success? Was she as repulsed as I am and wanted to get out? Or did she take the game too far? I tried to remain neutral, but my face gave my thoughts away.

"Bless you, Vicar, I have scandalised you!"

"Yes, I believe you have."

"The Aurora Agency is everything." *It sounded like a cult!* "For a few years, I happily dedicate myself to the company's success. In return, I am richly rewarded. One day, I will leave to follow my own dreams, as others have done before me. Until then, they supply *everything* I need to be the best."

"So, Steve wasn't joking when he spoke about selling your souls!"

Jenny snorted. "It's not forever! Just for a few years. And I can resign anytime I want to. It's only a job."

"It's intense."

"It's effective. It's brilliant. Aurora gets our best years creatively. They selected us for our ambition, our energy, and our talent. Celeste is a marketing genius. It is the ultimate apprenticeship."

Nothing ventured, nothing gained. "A dickie bird suggested that you and Celeste are, er, intimate?"

Jenny stiffened. I worried she had stopped breathing, then with one slow inward breath she regained her composure, though her light had dimmed. "I think that's enough idle gossip for one evening. Don't you, Vicar?"

"I'm sorry if I touched a nerve?"

"You are miles off touching anything," she replied. "Now, if you'll excuse me."

*Miles off? What could that mean?*

# And So To Bed

The hubbub of voices from the next room suggested most people were now heading to bed. I was in no rush to return. I wanted to take a beat to finish my tepid beverage and process all that had happened.

The Aurora Agency operated with a moral code that my 'parochial' mind struggled to fathom. There was a secret at its core. Something that everyone was doing their best to conceal. Did they all know what had happened to Ellen, or was there something else that they were hiding? For such a competitive company, they were very loyal to Steve and Celeste. This I found unusual. No one had moaned about their boss. I mean, I even complain about mine sometimes and He's the omnipotent, all-seeing creator of everything.

Shamefully, there are still times I question His mysterious ways. I am always wrong, of course, but it is human to wonder, to doubt.

When my coffee was too cold to remain pleasurable, I strolled out through the dining room to the terrace to see if I could find Lawrence. Perhaps he had discovered the key to this mystery during a conversation about football, or billiards, or whatever it is men bond over. I found him on the bench under the old oak tree. *Oh, tie a yellow ribbon round the... I have had way too much to drink.*

"Jess, my love, I thought you had retired already. Hugh was telling me about the time you smuggled him off the ferry dressed as a woman!"

"Yes, happy days!" I sighed. "I just came to say goodnight. Lawrence, *my love,* I wonder, if you might escort me to my room."

"Aye, aye," leered Hugh, his arm lazily wrapped around a sleeping Arabella. "Don't you two do anything naughty. I promised your parents, hic, sorry. I promised your... oh never mind. Have fun!"

"We will." I dragged Lawrence away from his newly found best friend.

"Will we?" Lawrence skipped beside me. "I thought..."

"Sssh, enough. You know the rules. Though in this house with its current guests, I think it's possible to have sex by osmosis!"

"Osmosis, that's hilarious. But I would, you know. I mean. I really love you, Jess. Like I *really* do."

"Well, then you can propose to me in the morning when you have sobered up."

"Will do, Vicar!" *Someone had thrown back a few too many Buck's Fizzes.*

\*\*\*\*\*

Lawrence walked with me back to my bedroom and left me with a sweet peck on the cheek. Arabella had put me in the Lilac Room, though the only reference to the colour or the flowers came in some prints hung above the bed. The rest of the decor played with various shades of cream and white, providing a blank canvas to set off the stunning Queen Anne style furniture. Each piece was delicately full-bodied, with curves in all the right places. In the centre stood a massive four-poster bed that could probably sleep a family of four without complaint. A silk nightdress and gown lay draped across it.

Teeth brushed and nightwear donned, Lawrence's promise spun around my head as the pillows swallowed me up. I think there are two schools of thought about drunken declarations of love. One, that they are the confused mumblings of a mind addled by alcohol and are not the true intentions of the person who uttered them. Or two, that the alcohol merely loosened their tongues, and what they said in that unguarded moment was very close to the truth in their heart.

If Lawrence loved me to the point of proposing, what would be my reply? We had only known each other a few months and had been dating even less. He was a kind, intelligent man. A man of honour, who had a strong moral code. He was attractive, in a gangly, fair-haired, nerdy kind of way. I enjoyed his company. He had a wonderful sense of humour. Though he could be reserved, he was not afraid of fighting for what he deemed important. And when he held me, butterflies danced in my heart. Did I love him? It was too soon to tell, surely? The first throes of a new relationship are often giddy affairs. One cannot base a future on them. *And yet?* He took my family and the witchy weirdness in his stride. He is actively encouraging my sleuthing, joining in, in fact. He is respectful. He is... He is... *Darn it! Now I can't sleep!*

I needed some hot milk or cocoa.

I grabbed the gown and snuck down to the kitchen.

*****

"Annie, are you still working?"

"Just preparing the breakfast things, Reverend Ward. Lovely to see you again. I hope you have had a good evening."

"Well, it's certainly been interesting. By the way, the food was gorgeous. You excelled yourself."

Annie loaded up the dumb waiter with clean crockery for the morning. "Oh, it's been a pleasure having guests to cater for. Just like the old days under Lord S. God rest his soul."

"I imagine you cooked for a strange array of characters back then."

"Oh, we've had all sorts here, Vicar. Pop stars, artists, politicians. You name them, they have probably been here for one of the master's parties. What these walls have seen and heard, if only they could talk." *I could only imagine!*

"I guess you and Ralph have seen and heard a few interesting titbits in your time too." I made helpful gestures, but Annie pointed at a wooden chair and invited me to sit down.

"My lips are sealed, though, of course."

"Of course."

"So, Vicar, is there something you wanted?"

"Yes, Annie. I can't sleep and I was going to help myself to some hot milk or a cup of cocoa."

"Then you stay seated right there and I'll put on the pan. I have Cadbury's, or Galaxy. That's a bit sweet for my tastes, but it's her ladyship's favourite. Or there's a Bourneville at the back somewhere."

"Ooh, Cadbury's would be wonderful. Thank you."

"My pleasure, in fact. Do you mind if I join you? Ralph is doing his last security check of the grounds. Checking in on the gate, etc. He'll still be some time."

"And that would be *my* pleasure."

Annie busied herself with mugs and milk whilst chatting away about all and sundry. I wanted to see if she had any interesting intel on their current guests.

"Hmm, this is just what the doctor ordered. Did I see you add double cream?"

"Of course. I forgot to ask. Would you like some of those mini marshmallows?" Annie rose, but I waved my hand for her to remain seated.

"Oh no, thank you. Much too sweet. This is absolutely perfect the way it is." After a few more minutes of general chit chat, I grasped my opportunity. "I shouldn't speak ill of my fellow dinner guests, but they are a strange bunch, don't you think?"

"No stranger than usual."

"But don't you think it's weird that they all are partying so hard after losing a member of their team so tragically?"

"Everyone grieves differently." She sipped her chocolate. "But there was one conversation I overheard... What time is it?" Annie looked at the clock on the wall behind me, "Yes, yesterday afternoon - between the two younger ladies and that black guy, on the main stairs." I tried not to respond negatively to how she described Archie. "Bit of a charmer, don't you think, Vicar?"

"Yes, he has a certain quality about him. What were they talking about?"

"I couldn't hear exactly. They kept their voices really low. I was hoovering the first landing, so missed a fair chunk of their conversation. They went quiet as I walked up past them to the plug socket on the next landing."

"So, what made you think it was strange?"

"Their body language, really. They were all hunched to-gether. You know, like rugby players in a scrum."

This piqued my curiosity. "What did you hear them say?" I cradled my drink between my palms and leaned forward, resting my elbows on the edge of the table to show I was hanging on her every word.

"Well," Annie mirrored me on the other side of the table. "The plump one with the pink hair, boy does she get dressed in the dark, anyway, she said something like 'we all need to stick together.'"

I took another sip of chocolate heaven. "And?"

"Then the guy said, 'you both promise you've got my back on this.'"

"Got his back? What could that mean?"

"Exactly. Anyway, then the prim one, you know the one with a broom up her backside. She began laughing really loudly, cackling, like a witch! So, I looked over the banister to check it out."

"What did you see?"

"Nothing, they must have turned away at the bottom of the stairs."

# Porridge and Kedgeree

Despite the delicious nocturnal elixir, I still tossed and turned in my oversized bed. I spent several hours tracing the pattern of the intricate lace canopy above my head, trying to puzzle out the design, and the clues I had gathered so far in this strange mystery. To be honest, the clues were few, and the questions were many. Hence my lack of sleep. I still didn't know if Ellen was murdered or not. The coroner may come to a different conclusion. *Poor Karen!* How was I to explain getting inebriated with her daughter's murderer, or murderers? Even if Ellen's death was an accident, there was something very wrong here. Very wrong indeed.

My mind refused to settle. When the dawn broke, I was pacing up and down the room. My spirit would not rest. As the bedside clock rolled its brass hands to six, I gave in to the sleepless night and took a shower instead. At seven, I walked down to the dining room. Ralph and Annie were putting out the crockery loaded into the dumb waiter the night before.

"You're early, Vicar!" Annie chirped. "You slept well then. Miraculous my hot cocoa, eh?" I didn't have the heart to tell her differently. "I have a special treat for the guests this morning. Them being Scottish and all that." She pulled back two hinged metal cloches on the side dresser. "This one's porridge and... this one's kedgeree."

"I'm sure they will appreciate it."

Annie bustled past to fetch more goodies from the kitchen. Ralph pulled out a chair for me at the table close to the bay window. "Would you prefer coffee or tea, Reverend Ward?"

"Oh, coffee, thank you. And, Ralph, can you make it extra, extra strong?"

"Of course. Please help yourself to some porridge, it will set you up for the day." *Even if the weather forecast is for another scorcher?* The sun was warming itself up for a long day of melting the earth below.

"I will. Thank you."

I breakfasted alone for nearly an hour. I was in no rush for company. Ralph and Annie fussed around me as they awaited the other guests. I felt like royalty.

Lawrence was the first to join me, but only briefly, as he had to rush to work. He swooped in, grabbed a bacon roll, placed a coffee-flavoured kiss on my lips and made me promise to call him after I met Karen at the coroner's office.

Next down were Hugh and Arabella, wrapped around each other like love-struck teenagers. There are many who would question the sensitivity of such a public display of togetherness so soon after her husband's death. But as I watched them gather their breakfasts from the extensive buffet, I thought how sad it was that they had felt obliged to hide their feelings for so long.

"Reverend, do you mind if we join you?" Arabella slid her bowl of fresh fruit along to the place-setting opposite mine.

"No, of course not. Though I will have to dash shortly to catch the ferry to the mainland."

"Of course, you are heading to Stourchester. Celeste mentioned that the poor girl's mother was an old friend. Wesberrey has a way of calling us back."

"Yes, I'm beginning to see that."

"Like the Hotel California," Hugh pulled out a chair beside Arabella and tucked a napkin into his shirt collar. "Don't want bacon grease on this," he explained. "I'm off to London. Audition. For a major Hollywood film."

"How wonderful. What do you mean 'Hotel California?'"

He nudged Arabella with his elbow. "Oh, you know. You can check out any time you like, but you can never leave. That's Wesberrey. There's no escape. Once she has you in her claws, she will always drag you back."

"Ha, yes. I get it. Any sign of your other guests?"

Arabella nibbled on a strawberry. "I think they had plans for an early morning swim before brekkie, but what time they would call early is anyone's guess. I'm only up because of this audition malarkey. Needed to make sure Hugh had a full stomach for the off."

"I told you to stay in bed. I'm a big boy, you know?"

"Oh, I know…" Arabella snatched a bite of air, prompting Hugh to offer her a fork full of bacon, which she leaned in to take. She licked her lips with more vigour than necessary for a Wednesday morning. Everyone in this house made me feel like I was playing gooseberry. *Time to make my excuses and leave!*

I returned to my room to collect my belongings and found my bed already made. *How did Annie and Ralph find the time?* I took a moment to check out the view from my window. The grounds, like the rest of Bridewell Manor, were quite magnificent. To my right stood the majestic branches of the old oak tree we had gravitated around during the evening. I looked down to see the terrace, a perfectly manicured lawn, and on my far left a glass structure that appeared to house the swimming pool. *Maybe next time?*

I paused for a quick word with the Boss. There was evil in this house. Behind all the partying and excess lay fragile people, who, like all of us, wanted to feel alive and feel love. For some, they find that in drunken parties and multiple partners, for others we find our solace in our faith and the closeness of those we love. I prayed for the occupants of Bridewell that they would find peace and happiness.

As I walked down the central staircase, I pondered on how my life had changed. This time last year, I was working in an inner-city parish in London organising Alpha courses for troubled youths. Now I was dining with the landed gentry and nursing champagne hangovers. What I wasn't doing was thinking about wedding proposals. Lawrence had obviously forgotten his midnight promise. A part of me was quietly disappointed.

"Help! Somebody call the police!"

"Someone, quick! It's Archie!"

I turned to see two bedraggled bathing beauties, water pooling on the marble floor at their feet.

"Ladies, calm down. What is the problem?"

Sweetpea rocked, her eyes glaring like a cartoon ghoul. "It's Archie, you know. In the pool. He's dead!"

# Happy Days

I doubt there are many Anglican vicars who have the head of homicide on their speed dial, but fortunately, I'm one of them. Annie brought warm towels to wrap around Sweetpea and Jenny's shivering bodies. As their screams had awoken the rest of the house, they were soon being comforted by Steve and Celeste in the breakfast room. The only person not accounted for, apart from Archie, was Captain Jack.

"I've checked his room, Ma'am, and there's no sign of the Captain or his things." Ralph stood tall to attention as he delivered the news to Arabella, falling on his army training to maintain proper order.

"Very well, Ralph." Lady Somerstone-Wright's thoughts switched to the comfort of her guests. "Can you ask Annie for some fresh coffee? Reverend Ward, did the Inspector indicate how long he would be?"

"No, but he is on his way." *Poor Arabella, not a happy end to her party.*

Hugh paced in front of the window. "Well, I hope he gets a move on. I can't keep Mr Howard waiting. He's not all 'Happy Days' now, you know."

"Darling, why don't you call your agent and explain."

"Explain what, my sweet? Sorry, but can you ask Ron to take the next flight back to L.A.? There's a dead man in my pool!"

"There, there, my love. This is very unfortunate."

"This was my big chance! Hollywood doesn't come knocking every day, you know." Hugh rounded on the other guests. "One of you did this! You ruined my chances. Your selfish, murdering ways have resigned me to BBC costume dramas for the rest of my days. You should have drowned me too!"

Arabella put a comforting arm around his waist and guided him to a box seat by the window. The rest of us remained as we were, frozen in shock. The truth was, though, that one of us probably was a ruthless killer.

Steve was the first to speak. "Where is the headmaster?"

"I imagine teaching year two. Anyway, Lawrence has nothing to do with this. What possible motive would he have, eh?"

"I wasnae accusing him of anything! For all we know, Archie had too much to drink and went for a late swim. This could be just another unfortunate accident." Steve pulled Sweetpea close against his chest, rubbing her towelled shoulders vigorously. "Shouldn't we let these poor lassies get dressed? They'll catch their deaths. Sorry, I didn't mean that. Sorry. This is all... it's all unbearable."

Ralph stepped forward to take command. "I think we should wait for the police. I can get a fire going if that will help?" Steve nodded. "Reverend, please ensure that no one leaves this room whilst I fetch some coal from the cellar."

My attention turned to Celeste and Jenny. Celeste was fussing with Jenny's damp, frizzy curls, detangling them with her long fingers and then smoothing them down. I wasn't sure what it was, but there was something particularly intimate about the gesture. Despite their denials, maybe Sweetpea was right about their relationship. Both the young women were sobbing, but I detected a wry smile on Jenny's face.

The doorbell rang. Hurried footsteps followed. The police had arrived.

*****

"Let me check I've got this right. You both held hands, ran, and dive-bombed into the pool without looking? And neither of you noticed Mr Baldwin's blood circling around you until you, Miss Brown, felt his hand brush your shoulder. Is that correct?"

The shivering duo nodded.

"You don't think that's extremely convenient?"

"I don't know what you mean, Inspector." Jenny pushed away from Celeste and uncurled herself. She swayed back and forth like a cobra. "We didn't see him from the doorway, that's all. He must have been floating in the left-hand corner."

Sweetpea whimpered, "I ran in with my eyes closed. When we came up for air, we were facing down the length of the pool and Archie swam in behind us, you know. Well, obviously he didn't swim, he floated, you know. But... argh, it was so horrible! Please, can I get dressed now?"

"I will let you know when you can go back to your room. PC Taylor is checking them out now."

The minutes ticked by. Inspector Lovington had no further questions. The forensics team and coroner were making their way across from the mainland, and for now, it was just a waiting game.

"Inspector, might I have a word?" I pulled Dave over to the bay window. "I need to catch a ferry and Hugh does too. I don't suppose you could let us go?"

"Jess, you are all either potential witnesses or suspects at this point. I'm sorry, but you will have to rearrange your appointments."

"I am meeting the first victim's mother in Stourchester, she's an old friend."

Dave rubbed his furrowed brow. "Of course she is. Now, why doesn't that surprise me? When and where?"

"Eleven o'clock. Outside the coroner's office. And I need to pick up Sam on the way."

"Dr Hawthorne knows her too? This gets better and better!"

"You know I had nothing to do with this. Neither did Mr Burton. He has a big audition with a Hollywood director in London. If you let him go now, it might just change his life." I tilted my head and did my very best puppy-dog impression.

"That doesn't work." He snapped his notebook shut.

"Sir! I've swept both bedrooms, there's no sign of any blood or a murder weapon."

"Thank you, constable. Will you escort the two ladies upstairs, please, and stand guard outside their rooms? I want their costumes bagged for the forensic team." Jenny helped her colleague to her feet. "Oh, and ladies, I want you both straight back down here. Do you hear me?"

"Loud and clear, Inspector. C'mon Sweetpea, let's get you tidied up."

"Mr Burton, I will expect you to report to the station in Stourchester first thing tomorrow morning to give your statement. If you fail to attend, I'm sure the press will be very interested. Need I say more?"

Hugh rushed across the room, clapping and bowing with gratitude. "Oh, thank you, thank you. I promise to give you tickets to the premiere."

Celeste tutted, "And the rest of us, Inspector. May we go too?"

"No, I'm afraid I will need to take all your statements first. Ralph, will you ask your wife to make everyone lunch?" Ralph clicked his heels and headed to the kitchen. "Now, Reverend, I will take your statement first, then you will be free to go."

"But I will be late!" I protested.

"Then I suggest you call Dr Hawthorne and get her to go ahead without you."

When Ralph returned, Dave instructed him to ensure no one else left the room. I suspected Ralph enjoyed his new role and the trust the Inspector placed in him. What I had learnt was that Ralph was a creature of duty and loyalty. No one would get past him.

Out in the hallway, as instructed, I called Sam and explained what had happened. "Right then, you want my statement. Shall we go to the sitting room?"

Dave pressed a finger into the bow of his pencil moustache. "No, I want you to come with me to the pool."

"Oh no, please, don't make me try to talk to Archie's sad departed spirit. I don't want to see him like that."

"Jess, please, I have nothing else to go on. Aren't you curious?"

"I'm not that curious!"

"Really?" His upper lip and eyelid twitched.

I sighed. "Lead on."

The sight of the young man's body floating face down in the water was thankfully less gruesome than I feared. There was a lot of blood, but then the water would make it spread and appear worse than it was. The source was a fearsome gash at the back of his head.

"Well, I think the cause of death is fairly obvious. What I need you to do is get some insights into who and how?"

"Really? I thought I was here to ask him about the weather!" I crouched down at the edge of the pool closest to Archie's right hand. "Do I need to worry about my fingerprints?"

"We'll take them later for elimination. Just get on with it, forensics will be here soon."

"I knew this wasn't kosher!" I stretched out my hand and grabbed at the fingers floating by. A heaviness formed in my chest. "He knew his attacker. I sense betrayal and confusion. He laughed and walked away. But they didn't hit him. I don't understand... he turned back. He wasn't afraid. I think it was an accident... did he fall?" I couldn't see anything other than a turquoise mist. "Blue. Everything is blue." I opened my eyes. "He was alive when he entered the pool."

"And a name? Did you see a face?"

"Sorry." I held my hand aloft. Dave took the cue and pulled me up.

"You wouldn't be holding out on me?" he asked.

"I thought you trusted me." I dried my hand on my top. "Now, can I leave?"

"I still need to get your statement."

"I didn't see or hear anything. There you go."

# Where Did The Day Go?

I ran back to the vicarage. Well, when I say I ran, I walked as fast as I could. I needed a change of clothes. Hugo was waiting on the front step. I scooped him up and squeezed him tight. I nuzzled his soft, black head. My eyes would stream, and my nose would be on fire for the next few hours, but it was worth it. I kept a firm grip on my furry friend as I searched for my keys and refused to let go all the way to the sofa in the morning room. He wriggled at first until he realised there was no escape. I don't recall the actual moment when it happened, but at some point, we lay down together and fell asleep.

My phone had fallen down the back of the sofa. The bugle ringtone woke me up, but I couldn't reach it before it went to voicemail. I had several missed calls from Sam, so I called her back straight away.

"Jess, why haven't you been answering your phone?"

"Sorry, I, er, fell asleep. Is Karen okay?"

"No, Jess, she's not. She's in absolute pieces and we have been hanging around here waiting for you to deign us with your presence."

"I said I'm sorry. I didn't sleep last night."

"Oh, and you think Karen did?" For a doctor, Sam was not good at dealing with people in distress.

"Where are you now?"

"At Oysterhaven, the ferry's due shortly."

"Okay, I will meet you on this side. We can go to the Cat and Fiddle for a drink and a spot of lunch."

"Lunch? Supper more like. Jess, do you know what time it is?"

*****

The daylight streaming through the curtains gave me no sign of the time, but my phone told me it was ten past three. I pushed Hugo off my lap and dashed upstairs to get dressed. Mum was still out, probably helping Rosie at the shop, so I put down some food for my new bestie. I opened the cabinet to pull out the medicine box to get my daily antihistamine fix and paused. I must have been asleep for four or five hours. *But I'm not sneezing. My eyes aren't red and itchy.*

"Hey, Hugo! I think I'm cured!" The hungry fluff ball was unimpressed and continued to lick the moist brown chunks in his bowl. "Right, well, I thought you would like to know. Guess we can stay housemates then. Catch you later, my furry friend."

I took the railway down to the harbour and waited for the ferry to dock. The quayside was bustling with tourists visiting the Regatta. I stood on a low wall close to the port to have a better vantage point. It would be easy to miss people in the crowd. Not that it was easy to miss Sam. She towered above the throng with her enormous straw hat. I waved furiously in her direction.

"Sam! Karen! Over here!" Once I was certain they had seen me, I carefully jumped down. The wall was only around three-foot-high, but I had always struggled with heights and now that I was older all sense of adventure has disappeared from such an activity. There was no challenge to it, only the genuine possibility of twisting my ankle.

I wouldn't have recognised Karen in a police line-up. The years had not treated her kindly. I remembered her as a sporty blonde with a tom-boyish streak, who loved skateboarding - when the boys allowed her. The American craze of the late Seventies had been a very gendered affair on Wesberrey, as it was in the whole of Britain. The girls had French skipping and the Double Dutch. Karen had excelled in both. The lady who stood before me now had her peroxide blonde hair scraped above her head in a severe ponytail. Her sagging skin bore a fake tan, her crayoned eyebrows mirrored the dark circles beneath. The crepey lids in between hooded, weary, tear-stained eyes. Our greeting was a sober affair.

"Karen, I am so sorry about Ellen and missing you this morning. I hope Sam explained what happened."

"She did."

I stepped forward to offer a hug but thought better of it. "Have you eaten? The pub's packed, but we know the owner. I am sure he will squeeze us in if we ask nicely."

"This place hasn't changed a bit." Karen sniffed "Still a dump."

"It's really not that bad."

Sam rolled her eyes at my misplaced attempts to be jolly. "Come on, you've been travelling all night and need to relax. Then we'll get a taxi up to the vicarage. Jess, I thought I would stay the night to help Karen settle in if that's okay with you?"

"The more the merr..." *The more the merrier? Jess Ward, have you lost your mind?* "Of course. Mum will love to see you both. Just like old times."

"Except, it ain't."

"No, Karen. Except it ain't." I opened my arms and waited for her to accept me. For an awkward moment, the world went into slow motion. Her pain sent ripples through the air, turning everything it touched grey. There was no more sun. No more time. Just grief.

Sam stepped in to fill the void. Stretching her long arms around us both, she pulled us together. "The Wesberrey Angels are back together." Snotty, red-eyed, tear waterfalls streamed down the wrinkles of the past forty years.

Karen took a small step back, wiped her nose on her sleeve, and slapped me and Sam on our backs. "To the pub!"

"To the pub!"

*****

"You haven't changed a bit, you know." Karen had ordered gammon and chips with a large pint of lager.

"Neither have you." I lied.

"Rubbish! I look like my mum. The only thing missing is the cigarette hanging from my lip and the floral pinny."

"I liked your Mum," Sam played with her beer mat, flipping it up from the table's edge and catching it. "She was a good, hard-working woman."

"She had no choice. Dad was a waste of space. Trust me to marry a sod just like him."

I remembered her husband had died only a few years ago. "I understand from Sam, that he passed away."

"Yes, well, that's life, isn't it?" Karen diverted her attention to the crowds in the street outside. "So, you both came back here. Done well for yourselves, haven't you? Fancy doctor, a priest. Strange world, eh?"

The conversation stalled. What could we talk about? It was hardly the time to reminisce about old times, or even to catch up with funny anecdotes about our adventures in the years we'd been apart. The only reason we were back together was because Karen's only child had died in the waters that encircled us. I wanted to find out what the coroner had said. But I had to be patient. I had never been more grateful to see Phil's arms full of pub grub.

Karen took the ketchup bottle from the condiment holder and smothered her plate with tomato sauce. The pineapple rings on her bacon steaks disappeared in a sea of red. Images of Ellen's mangled corpse floated in and out of my mind. That was no way to remember my friend's daughter. "Do you have a picture of Ellen?" I asked.

"Uh-huh." Karen pulled out a photograph from her purse of a pretty blonde teenager lounging on a deck chair. It could have been a picture of Karen when she was younger, but it was Ellen.

"May I?" I took the corner and brought it closer. "She looks like you. She was very beautiful."

"Aye, and clever too." Karen's loving words drifted away. Ellen's voice took their place.

*"Tell her I love her. And I'm sorry for causing her pain."*

"She says she loves you."

"She what?"

"And she's sorry for causing you so much pain."

"Jess, this isn't funny!"

Sam's arm folded around our friend "She's a Bailey, re-member. Jess has the gift."

*"Tell her, I got her present, at Christmas. That I meant to call and thank her."*

"She is asking me to tell you she meant to call. That she got your Christmas present."

"What? Is that really Ellen? Jess? If it's her, what did I send her?"

*"Britney. It was a Britney Spears doll, I had always wanted one."*

"A Britney Spears doll?"

"Oh, my God! I found it on eBay!" Karen squealed. "Can she see me? Is she here?" She squeezed Sam so hard with excitement, "Jess, tell Ellen I love her."

I didn't need to. I knew she could hear, and I knew what she wanted me to say next.

"She knows. And don't worry. She is at peace now."

# You Have One Shot

After two nights straight of excessive alcohol consumption, I had ordered orange juice to go with my meal. Now I needed a stiff drink. "Karen. Sam. I'm sorry, will you excuse me?"

This whole sixth sense thing was freaking me out. I staggered to the bar and ordered a rum and coke before slipping away to the relative peace of the Ladies' room. Ellen's spirit had left as quickly as it arrived. I punched the flimsy wall of the toilet stall. *You stupid, stupid fool! You should have asked her. You blew it!*

There was only one woman who could help me get a handle on all of this. I opened my phone's address book and dialled. "Aunt Cindy? Are you free to talk?"

*****

When we arrived at the vicarage, we found the 'Charmed', aka Mum, Cindy, and Aunt Pamela, huddled around the kitchen table.

"Mum, you remember Karen?"

"Of course, dear. I am so sorry for your loss. Why don't the three of you join Hugo in the front? We'll be along later. I brought back some vegan carrot cake from the bookshop. Would you like a slice, with a cup of tea?"

"Were they casting spells?" Karen asked as she settled down on the sofa. "Mum used to say your family were witches. I never believed her, of course."

"You knew more about my family than I did then." I lifted Hugo up from his spot on the two-seater. "Why didn't you ever say anything?"

"You might have turned me into a toad!" Karen shuffled down the sofa to make room for Sam. "I remember one time your Mum made us tapioca pudding and joked it contained real frog spawn. I passed, just in case. Think I said I was still full from lunch or something."

"Yuk. I hated desserts back then. Do you remember school custard?" Sam plumped up a cushion against the arm of the couch and swung up her long legs along its length, pushing Karen even further down the other end. "The chocolate one was the worst, with the skin on the top? Put me off chocolate flavoured things for life!"

"You don't like chocolate? You aren't even human." Karen shunted back along, reclaiming her spot. Their behaviour was playful. It brought back so many happy memories.

"Oh, I love chocolate, just not chocolate-flavoured things. Except for liqueurs. I am rather partial to chocolate liquor."

"You're rather partial to anything with alcohol." Hugo circled and clawed at my lap. *Still no sneezing!* "Karen, Sam here has a filing cabinet full of booze in her office."

"For medicinal purposes only, I guess," Karen joked.

"All donations from grateful patients," Sam replied.

At that moment, Mum pushed open the door with a tray of tempting goodies. Her sisters filed in behind with teapots, cups, and saucers.

"Hubble, bubble, toil and trouble," I mumbled. Mum didn't hear me, but my friends did, and we descended into a childish fit of giggles.

It was good to see Karen smile. It's a strange thing about grief. We think it's a constant, a continuous emotion, but most of us seek opportunities to ease the tension. It's the only way to survive. Humour and death may appear strange bedfellows, but they are frequent ones. In my job, I have comforted many a grieving soul and regularly seen people switch from laughter to tears and back again. They can also move from sadness to anger, or from hyper-busy to catatonic. There is no right way, only your way. Karen's way was to soldier on.

Mum sat beside me. Pamela took the winged back chair by the fire. Cindy crossed her legs and eased herself onto the rug at her feet. Sam offered to swap places, but Cindy was happy on the floor. *If I'm going to inherit her superpowers, could that include her suppleness too?*

"Right, my darlings." Cindy raised her arms in a circular motion, joining them above her head. She brought them down, and they rested, ready for prayer, in front of her chest. "Jess, do you want to do the honours?"

"To do the what now? Oh, you want me to, er... okay." I watched my friends and family hold hands. "I'm sure the Boss is in." I cleared my throat. "Our Saviour said that whenever two or three are gathered in his name, he is here in our midst. We thank him for gathering us here this evening. Let us ask for his guidance so that we can support our sister, Karen. In God's name, we pray that her daughter, Ellen, is resting safely in his mercy. We trust that a mother's grieving heart can find comfort in the love we all share. Amen."

Everyone muttered, "Amen".

"Right," Mum's voice broke through the silence, "Who wants cake?"

*****

Cake was only an appetiser. Mum had planned out a three-course dinner and insisted that we ate in the dining room and use the best china. I volunteered myself and

Cindy for the task, and took the opportunity to grab a few minutes alone with my ethereal aunt.

"Well?"

"Well what, darling child?"

"You know exactly why I invited you up here and it wasn't so you could put me to shame with your yoga moves!"

"Jessie, darling, you are still resisting, aren't you? I understand. It takes time."

"No, it takes explanation. Guidance. You only speak in riddles and that doesn't cut it when I have dead people having full-blown conversations with me. Please, I want to help my friend."

Cindy patted my hand, "And that's very commendable of you."

I wanted to swear. I burst into tears instead. "I should have asked Ellen how she died. She had the chance to tell me, why didn't she?"

Cindy walked to the cupboard and collected six crystal glasses. "Because it wasn't important to her." She slid one glass to the right of the place setting opposite me.

"Knowing how she died. Telling us who killed her, isn't important?"

Cindy glided along the table as she continued to put out the other glasses. "Will it change anything?" She paused. "Will it bring her back?"

"No, of course not." I dried my face on my sleeve. "But…"

"But what? Ellen wanted to tell her mother that she loved her. They were estranged when she died, weren't they? We always think there is time. When we find out there isn't, it is the things we didn't say that matter the most. She had one shot, and she took it."

"One shot?"

"You hadn't slept much. You were tired, emotional, and your guard was down. If you could only learn to relax, more would be revealed."

"So, you don't think Ellen will come back?"

"No, my darling one, she has made her peace. Now, you have to find yours."

# Unfortunate Accidents

As I sat opposite Karen at dinner, I was a mess of emotions. Part of me was relieved that I had offered Ellen a chance to say goodbye. Part of me felt guilty that I was no closer to knowing what had happened. And now there had been a second death. Could it be possible for both young people to meet with tragic accidents? That would be unfortunate in the extreme, but I had no evidence to suggest otherwise. There were no physical clues, and the psychic insights I had received told me absolutely nothing. I had learnt that the coroner's report was inconclusive, and they were doing more tests, so that didn't help. Though I doubted Archie's death was accidental, it was still possible. All I had to go on was my instinct that the others were hiding something and Annie's partially overheard conversation. Captain Jack's disappearance was interesting, though. Perhaps all will be revealed when the police find him. Where was he, and why did he run?

A dramatic knock on the door interrupted my musings. Mum was the first up and motioned to the rest of us to stay seated.

"Zuzu! What a pleasant surprise! Dave, are you still on duty? Come through, we're having dinner." The golden couple had arrived. "Karen, you must remember Jess's older sister Susannah?" Karen nodded. "And this is Chief Police Inspector Dave Lovington. I believe he is heading up Ellen's case." What little colour remained on my friend's face drained at the mention of her daughter's name. Mum continued, unperturbed. "You must both join us for a bite to eat. There is plenty to go around."

Dave ran an awkward finger around his shirt collar. "I need to speak to Mrs Findlay as soon as possible."

Cindy flicked her hair and fixed him with a mesmerising stare. "Dave, darling, surely it can wait an hour. Sit. Eat. Karen isn't going anywhere." Dave caved and pulled out a chair at the table end where my efficient mother had already started laying out silver cutlery. Cindy's ability to get Dave to do her bidding without question never failed to impress me.

The conversation tiptoed around the humongous elephant in the room - Ellen and Archie's deaths. We talked about the weather. It had been crazy hot. The impending nuptials on Saturday, how stunning Barbara was going to look and how funny it was that she was so nervous. Zuzu spoke about how quickly Amazon had delivered her Marilyn Monroe dress, especially considering we are offshore. And Pamela repeatedly reminded us she had spoken to Hugh Burton on the phone and how gracious he had been to her. *What a gentleman!*

Finally, with all food and conversation exhausted, Dave asked if he could use my study to interview Karen. I agreed on condition that I could accompany my old friend.

I pulled across a second chair for Karen at the front of my desk and sat as close to her as possible. The inspector sat resolute in my office chair. Karen held my hand. I was tempted to close my eyes and try to tune into her, but it would be rude to go there uninvited.

"Dear Mrs Findlay, I am deeply sorry for your loss. I will keep this as short as possible. You must be exhausted after your long journey."

"I suppose I must be." Karen shook her head and shoulders. There's an expression people use when they feel a cold shudder, that 'someone is walking on their grave'. Maybe they were. Karen's hand was clammy, her features ghostly. She didn't look at the inspector directly but maintained a steady gaze aimed nowhere in particular.

Dave pressed on. "When did you last speak to your daughter?"

She jerked her head from side to side as if the memory was stuck in a pinball machine. "Must have been last summer."

Dave glanced up from his notepad. "*Last* summer?"

Karen's hand flinched in mine. "Yes, I know what you're thinking. I think it too."

"Mrs Findlay, Ellen had only worked for the Aurora Agency for six months. Did you know anything about that?"

"Like I said, Inspector, I haven't spoken to my daughter in over a year. I'm afraid there is very little I can tell you. The last time we spoke she was working in the HR department of a merchant bank in Canary Wharf. I didn't even know she'd moved back to Scotland." Her voice trailed off. "I sent her Christmas present to her old workplace. I guess they must have forwarded it to her. How kind of them."

"Mrs Findlay, I have to ask. Why did you and your daughter stop talking?"

"I can't remember. I must have upset her somehow, but I don't know what I did." Karen's fingernails dug deep. "I really don't know what I did wrong, Jess."

"I know." The pain from her nails piercing my skin was nothing to the turmoil in her heart. I patted her hand. "Do you remember what you spoke about?"

"Normal stuff. How she was. What she was doing. She just said she was okay and there was nothing new. She wasn't particularly happy with her job. I guess she decided to move on." Sobs crowded out what she said next, but I guessed it was something like why didn't she tell me.

Dave shifted to the edge of his chair. "Mrs Findlay, did Ellen suffer from depression, or anxiety to your knowledge?"

"She wouldn't have killed herself, Inspector!" Her nails gripped tighter. "Suicides blame themselves, don't they? They believe the world would be better off without them. They internalise the hurt. My daughter was one of those people who blamed their troubles on the world. There is no way she ended her own life. My baby always put herself first. And that was one of the things I loved most about her. She didn't suffer fools. Ellen had a strong sense of justice. She was strong and beautiful. She was my warrior princess."

Karen folded into my arms. "I think you have all you need, Dave." I stroked her ponytail. "My friend needs to rest."

*****

Once Zuzu and Dave had left, I helped Karen up to her room. Sam was going to sleep in Rosie's old room again, so Mum had prepared Zuzu's former crash pad for our latest guest. Sometime during the past twenty-four hours, as well as cooking a three-course meal and baking at my sister's shop, Mum had changed the bed linen, deep cleaned the entire room, and even put out fresh flowers. *What would I do without her?* Karen moved the pile of clean towels off the bed onto a nearby dresser and curled up on top of the duvet. Mum had opened the window to air the room out, so I went over to close it.

"No, Jess, leave it open."

"But the forecast was for a break in the weather today, there might be a storm during the night."

"I know. I like to hear the thunder. And, at our age, you know, hot flushes and all that."

"I hear you!" I nudged my rear end onto the bed beside her and rubbed her back. "You can stay here as long as you need to, okay? Sam's across the way and I'm just a few doors down. We're here for you."

"I know. Thank you. You have both been very kind." As she spoke, Karen's spirit faded into the mattress beneath her. She wasn't relaxing, just giving up. "Jess?"

"Yes, what is it?"

"Will you pray for me?"

"Of course, I will."

And I did.

# Quid Pro Quo

"Jess, I was thinking. Would you agree to bury Ellen with my mother in the churchyard?" Karen was much restored after her sleep and was tucking into a heaving plate of poached eggs and crispy bacon.

"I am sure that can be arranged. You don't want to take her back with you to Scotland?"

"I'm not sure I want to go back. There's nothing there for me. Just a council flat and a treasure chest of unhappy memories."

Sam kept looking at her watch, torn between being there for her friend and needing to be back at the hospital for her rounds. "Then why don't you move back here?"

"Maybe." Karen picked up a thin bacon slice with her fingers and dangled it in front of her mouth. "I can claim Universal Credit the same here as anywhere."

Sam offered our grieving friend a paper towel from the cupboard to wipe her greasy fingers. "I'm sorry. I have to dash but hold that thought. I'm sure we can get you a job or something." She stood to kiss Karen on the head and turned to leave.

"You've never kissed me goodbye." I quipped.

"Boy, you're needy," she flounced around the table and planted a giant smacker in the middle of my forehead.

Mum emerged from the fridge with fresh milk for the second pot of tea brewing on the table. "Jess needs a housekeeper."

"That's a great idea. I can pay you out of the parish funds and you could live here, or find your own place, or..."

"I'll think about it." *Smart, I probably should too... who eats bacon with their fingers?*

A few mouthfuls of toast later, my mobile rang.

It was Dave.

"Excuse me, I'll take this in my office." I hurried along the corridor. Sensitive to being overheard, I firmly shut the office door. "Any news?"

"We've found Captain Jack. You need to drop whatever vicary thing you are doing right now and get down here. The *Captain* says he will only talk if *you're* present. PC Taylor is holding him in the back room of the Cat and Fiddle."

"I'm on my way."

*****

Jumping on Cilla, I stuffed my pack-a-mac into my rucksack. The predicted storms had held off during the night, but the weather reporter still forecasted heavy rains during the day. Suitably equipped for an English summer, I raced down to a bustling Market Square.

There was a clear increase in police presence on the island. Usually, PC Taylor was the only uniform in sight. Now there were officers talking to people around the ferry, outside the shops and market stalls and along the seafront. Dave was waiting for me at the pub's entrance.

"I have a few rules," he said. "We suspect Jack Shipton murdered Ellen Findlay and Archie Baldwin. I need you to get him to confess. We found him trying to get away on the *Norma Jean* around two am this morning. Don't let him fool you, he's a highly dangerous individual." *Or a frightened one.*

"So, what are the rules?"

"Think Hannibal Lecter. No touching, sit at least two metres apart and don't give any personal information."

"Just call me Clarice!" I said, channelling my inner Jodie Foster.

"This is no joking matter."

"Dave, I can handle myself. Will you or PC Taylor be in the room with me?"

"Of course."

"Then I think I'll be safe." I brushed an imaginary piece of fluff from Dave's jacket. "Let's do this. I'm a busy woman."

*****

I did my best not to let my smugness tease the corners of my mouth too much. I knew Captain Jack's requests were grinding the Inspector's gears, and I admit I was enjoying every moment. As I strolled past a table full of uniformed officers grabbing a late breakfast in the saloon bar, my instinct told me that Captain Jack was not a threat. It was curious how he wanted to talk to me and not the police alone. Our earlier conversation on the bench might hold a clue. He had warned Archie not to trust the coppers, and maybe he wanted an independent witness. He should have asked for his lawyer, of course. There was only Ernest on the island, but they could bring one from the mainland in a few hours.

I pushed through the backroom door to see the captain handcuffed to a chair marooned in a sea of billowy white. The room was being decorated for Saturday's wedding reception. I am not sure that the decor gave any clues to what Barbara will wear down the aisle, but there was a lot of white lace, orange blossom and fairy lights. PC Taylor stood on guard in the far corner by the door to the kitchen.

"Okay, Shipton, I brought the vicar." Dave stood square on, arms folded across his chest, and grunted. "Now, will you tell us how you killed Miss Findlay and Mr Baldwin?"

"Nope!" The captain stared the inspector down.

"Why not, man?"

"Because I didn't do it, *man!*"

Dave's temple vein twitched with frustration. "Shipton, you tried to steal away in the middle of the night."

The captain remained steadfast. "Yes, Inspector, there's a killer on the loose. Wouldn't you try to get as far away as you could too?"

This Mexican stand-off was getting us nowhere. "Captain Jack, you asked for me to be here. May I ask why?"

"Because, Reverend Ward, the boys in blue just want a quick win. They have no evidence, but they seem convinced they have their man."

"Is that the only reason?" I suspected he knew more than he was saying.

Now it was Captain Shipton's turn to look smug. "What if I knew why?"

Dave paced around the chair. "Then you should stop playing games."

"I will if you remove the handcuffs and talk to me as an equal."

Dave had an iron will. I determined to bend it a little with some feminine logic. "Inspector, the pub and Market Square beyond are teeming with police. You and PC Taylor are both in here. I am sure you could easily overpower this old man if he tried to make a break for it."

"Eh, Vicar, not so much of the old. But she is right, Lovington, how far would I get with half of Stourchester's finest between me and the *Norma Jean*? And on market day too. Have you seen how busy it gets?"

Dave signalled to PC Taylor to remove the cuffs.

"There, that's better." I soft clapped my appreciation. "Captain Jack, are you hungry? Thirsty? I'll ask Phil for the brunch menu, then we can talk."

*****

Three builder's cups of tea and a sausage sandwich smothered in HP sauce later, Captain Jack was ready to 'spill the beans'. He rolled back in his chair and wiped traces of the brown condiment from his beard with a napkin.

"There's a diary."

I still had a few sips of tea left in my cup. I took one before replying. *I don't want to appear too excited.* "Whose diary?"

"That Ellen Findlay's, of course." Jack threw down the napkin in triumph. "She had quite a love of secrets."

"Do you have it?"

"Nope, but I know who took it."

We waited. Jack was milking his moment to the fullest.

I caved, "Well, who took it?"

"Archie. It was his special mission." Jack leaned forward and rubbed his beard. "You know, all that tea has left a sour taste in my mouth. I don't suppose a drop of rum would be permissible?"

Dave's furious breath blew across my shoulder. "Enough stalling. This diary doesn't prove your innocence if it even exists,"

"Oh, it exists, Inspector. I saw it."

"And did you get to read inside?"

"Maybe? As I said, I'm getting a powerful thirst." Jack shrugged. "We are in a pub, for heaven's sake. You are torturing me here!"

Dave pushed past me and grabbed the table. "Speak first. If what you have to say is worth my time, PC Taylor here will get you your drink."

"Hmm, I suppose that's a fair compromise. Wouldn't want you lot in court to say I was being uncooperative." Jack drummed his fingers on the table, tilted his head towards me, and smirked. "*They* asked Archie to borrow her diary. *They* told him it was a prank. So, he wormed his way into her bedroom and stole it away whilst she showered."

"Who are *they*?" I asked.

"Now, that I don't know, but there are only four potential suspects. I'll leave the detecting to someone else."

Dave huffed. This game of cat and mouse was testing his patience. "And you definitely saw this diary?"

"Yes, Archie wanted my advice. You see, he thought it would be all girly, you know. All rainbows and unicorns. Reflections on the day and hopes for the future, maybe a few sexual fantasies, you know the sort of stuff."

"And it wasn't?" My knowledge of Ellen so far didn't suggest she was a unicorn type of girl.

"Nope. It read like a military battle plan. There were objectives and targets. And she wrote a lot in code. Poor Archie was a bit spooked by it, to be honest. He was going to put it back."

Dave's mood mellowed. "Then what stopped him?" It was a redundant question. We both knew the answer.

"Well, she turned up dead," Jack replied.

"Do you know where the diary is now?"

The captain breathed deeply and turned away. A tear clung to his lower lash. "Reverend, I sorely wish I did." He spat out the rest of his sentence through clenched teeth. "Because the bastard who has it now killed my first mate to get it."

# Green Ice Cream

With a lawyer on the way, we left the captain downing a tumbler of rum under the officious eye of PC Taylor.

"Don't you think it's time you made him a sergeant?" I whispered, as we walked back into the main bar.

"It's not down to me. Anyway, he says he has a phobia of exams." Dave led me back out in the refreshing midday sun. "Fancy a stroll along the front?"

There was a time my heart would have done somersaults at such a suggestion. "What are you going to do with the captain? He can't go back to Bridewell."

"No. I don't want him free to roam, either. Maybe I'll put him under boat arrest. Station a few officers there and take away the keys."

"Do you still think he did it?"

Dave paused. His eyes scanned the horizon as the wheels spun inside his head. "The diary might be a brilliant invention to deflect us away from his guilt. No one else has mentioned it."

"Well, they wouldn't, would they? I mean if they were the murderer. Maybe only the killer knew of its existence." I thought it was a good time to mention the conversation Annie had overheard on the stairs. My retelling ended just as we drew near to an ice cream stall. "Ooh, they have pistachio! I haven't had that since I was a kid." *Probably from the same stall.*

"And, if I buy you a cone, will you promise to tell me everything else you have discovered?" My inner child cried yes. *I scream, you scream, we all scream for ice cream!* Dave bought a double scoop of chocolate and raspberry ripple from the straw-hatted vendor for himself and a green stack of mint and pistachio for me. We planted ourselves on a nearby wall to enjoy their frozen creamy goodness.

"Jess, you must tell me when you learn something new. And getting Lawrence involved in your amateur sleuthing too." He tutted, "Archie might not have been the only one floating in that pool."

"I know. I will be more careful in the future."

A thin ice cream coating softened the line of his pencil moustache. I knew what his lips were about to utter. "Jess, there will be no 'in the future', do you understand? I was wrong to get you involved at all. This is my case. It's not like I can use anything you discern from your 'gift' in court, anyway. The rest would be hearsay. I need evidence. I need to find that diary *if* it exists."

"Then, let me help." I focused on my ice cream to avoid his glare and pressed on. "I can go back to Bridewell. Say I left something behind and search the place. No one's been allowed to leave. I mean, they have had hours to get rid of it, but it has to still be on the grounds, somewhere."

Dave took a long, pensive lick of his cone and gazed at the sparkling water in front. "*If* I let you go back there. And it's a big if. You aren't to talk to any of the guests. And you touch nothing. Just alert me to what you find, and I will send in an officer to collect it. Do you understand?"

"Inspector Lovington, I always understand."

"To be clear, I am only sending you in so that they, whoever *they* are, don't suspect we are looking for the diary. If my officers rummage through their drawers, the culprit might get wind and panic. I don't want more dead bodies on my conscience."

"Understood. Only one question? Can I finish my ice cream first?"

He grinned, "And this is absolutely the very last time ever you play detective."

"Scout's honour!"

"Were you ever a scout?" Dave wiped his moustache and smiled.

"No, but I was a brownie for a few months. Does that count?"

\*\*\*\*\*

The inspector phoned ahead to warn one of his officers stationed at Bridewell Manor that I was coming and to allow me free access to the house. I left him at the pub and climbed aboard Cilla for the short uphill drive to Upper Road via Abbey View Drive. As they had done in my youth, children were riding their bikes and skateboards down its steep incline in the summer sun. I remembered how Karen used to love to hang out with the skater boys. *Such innocent, carefree times.*

I found a police officer manning the security gate. A quick flash of my white clerical collar and he buzzed me through. Ralph greeted me as I approached the main entrance.

"Reverend, I thought you would have stayed a million miles away from here, given what's happened."

"I lost my, er, phone. I think I must have dropped it somewhere. What with all the chaos yesterday morning and stuff. Inspector Lovington said I could look in my room."

"Be my guest, Reverend Ward. Did the inspector tell you how much longer he is going to hold people here? Everyone's getting cabin fever." I suggested that people would be free to roam once the forensics team had finished their job. "It was like being in prison, Reverend. Anyway, must be done, I suppose. You know the way. I would escort you, but Annie is ready to serve lunch. Between you and me, she's a little overwrought by all that's been going on. She cares so much for her ladyship, you know. We so wanted this impromptu dinner party to be a success. Encourage Lady Arabella to do some more entertaining. Like in the old days."

"Well, the party was a tremendous success." I reassured him, "It was the morning after that wasn't quite to plan. None of you are to blame for that."

"But I should have checked the pool. After we heard the commotion. I mean, I was just so tired. Neither of us are as young as we once were, Reverend. And we're not used to it. Having guests here, that is. It's usually only us and Ms Arabella. Sometimes Master Tristan. Mr Burton has been away filming a lot since His Lordship passed."

I had to rewind the conversation a smidgeon. "What commotion?"

"It would have been around three in the morning. There were loud voices coming from the pool area. Our bedroom is at the front, to the side. There are not a lot of soft furnishings in that part of the house. Sound carries."

"Did you hear what they were discussing?"

"It didn't sound much like a discussion. I could tell one of them was the Jamaican guy by his accent. His voice boomed through the walls. I swear he was laughing, though. You know, playing around. I think the other voices were female, but I could be wrong. There was a splash, but I thought they were larking about in the pool. How was I to know it was more sinister than that?"

I placed a comforting arm around his sturdy frame. "There was no way you could or should have suspected anything other than a bit of high jinks. We had all had a lot to drink."

"Yes, Reverend. Anyway. I hope you find your phone. You can see yourself out afterwards?"

"My pho- yes, yes, my phone. Of course. You are very busy, Ralph. And please don't worry. Just a suggestion, though. I think you should tell one of the police officers what you heard *after* lunch. It might be important." *That should give me enough time to safely search the bedrooms.*

I knew everyone was downstairs, but my heart was still firmly in my throat as I pushed against the first bedroom door. The mix of male and female clothes scattered on the bed and draped over the dressing table chair told me I was in Steve and Celeste's room. Their bed looked untouched, apart from the clothes and slightly ruched sheets. It had been a warm night. Perhaps they had slept on top of the covers. The disarray seemed out of character. I had expected Celeste to treat her wardrobe with more respect, and Steve didn't come across as a man who tolerated mess and disorder. *They had just lost a beloved employee! Maybe they had other things on their mind. Yes, like getting their hands on her diary!*

I dug out the last of the plastic gloves from my trouser pocket and pulled them on. I pulled out empty drawers, searched under the bed, in the folds of the curtains. I even took the lid off the cistern of their ensuite toilet, but everywhere came up empty. My last hope was the desk in the corner. Nothing again, other than a slim brown folder poking out from under the leather-bound blotting-pad. *Curiouser and curiouser.* Inside was a thirty-year-old letter in French dated the '22 Mars' of that year, and a second document titled 'Déclaration de Naissance'.

Even my limited French worked out that this was the birth certificate for a baby girl born a few days earlier on the eighteenth of March. The baby's name was Guenièvre. The space for her father's name was blank. Her mother was Celeste Marron.

*Celeste had a child!*

\*\*\*\*\*

I tucked the folder back under the pad. The logical half of my brain was telling me 'so what?' Celeste had a child thirty years ago. It was very unlikely to have any bearing on the current case. I knew Ellen wasn't her daughter unless she was adopted? I never thought to ask Karen. *Well, you don't as a matter of course, do you?* Being Celeste's love child would explain a lot. It would explain why she went for the job at Aurora and didn't tell her mother about it. It would explain secret coded entries in her diary, if it existed, of course. And it would explain her desire to use Archie to find out more information if that is actually what I channelled in her cabin.

There were a lot of 'ifs' and this was wild speculation. I had no evidence that Ellen was Celeste's daughter. I could ask Karen, but how would I introduce it into the conversation? *Her password!* If the date used on her laptop was the eighteenth of March, that would prove it! I made a mental note to call Dave with this idea as soon as I was back outside.

I did my best to leave everything as I had found it and sneaked along the corridor to the next room along. The bright pink wig resting on a polystyrene head on the dresser told me I had found Sweetpea's boudoir. *So, she doesn't dye her hair.* Her suitcase revealed several more coloured wigs of various lengths and hues safely stowed in fabric drawstring bags. The wardrobe was a floral sensation packed with a kaleidoscope of ditsy dresses and jackets.

On her desk sat a stack of papers and a rose gold laptop. It was ordered chaos. Initially, her belongings appeared to be a full-on assault on the senses, yet on closer inspection, each had a use and a logical place. I pulled out every drawer and squeezed my hand into every nook and cranny, but there was no diary. *This is a wild goose chase!*

Next door was Jenny's room, and it looked exactly as I expected - tidy to the point of obsessive compulsion. You could have bounced a coin off the tautness of the bedsheets. *I'm sure I saw that in an old war movie, or was it 'Private Benjamin'?* She had a neat stack of coloured folders on the desk, all carefully labelled. There was nothing of interest inside any of them unless you had some weird fetish for excel spreadsheets and bar charts. Her black laptop was locked, as was the desk drawer underneath it. *Strange, none of the others had locked theirs.* Of course, that didn't mean the diary was in it. For starters, was there even a key? None of the other desks had one. The drawer may have been locked already or stuck shut. I tried to jimmy it open, but it would not budge. Short of breaking it, I couldn't find a way in.

The only other possibility was that it was still in Archie's bedroom. I needed to get a move on. Lunch would be over soon. I found Archie's things gathered in the centre of the room. It looked like the police had already searched here. *But they weren't looking for a lady's diary!* I flicked through his bags and checked the desk and the bathroom. Nothing. I smoothed my hands over the bedcovers and underneath the pillows. More nothing. I went through drawers and pulled open cupboard doors. Even more nothing. Then I noticed that his room had wooden shutters pushed back to let in the day. I unfolded the panel nearest to the bed... *Voila!* A slim peach gold embossed journal fell to the floor.

This was Ellen's diary, just as Jack had described it. I closed my eyes and breathed deeply. If Ellen was planning on making a return visit, now would be a good time to call. After a few minutes, I gave up. *The psychic hotline must be down for maintenance.* The journal entries were mostly in code, and way above my level of intelligence to decipher. *I can't even make above four-letter words in Scrabble.* The quicker the police boffins got their smart hands on this treasure, the better. *Just take a few photographs first, aren't smart phones wonderful things!* Photos taken, I slipped the diary back behind the panel and made good my escape.

Almost.

The second my foot touched the marble floor at the foot of the stairway, my wonderful phone rang. It was Lawrence. I hit 'decline', checked to see if anyone was around, and made a bolt for the door. Once I had Cilla back on the main road, I pulled over to make two important calls. One to Inspector Lovington to advise him where to find the diary and suggest a possible password, and the other? To apologise to Lawrence for not calling him earlier and putting the phone down on him. *It's a good thing he loves me.*

# Princess Of Pop

I arranged to pop over to see Lawrence after the school day had finished, but first I wanted to check up on Karen. I knew Mum would make sure she was fed and watered. It was my job to keep her company. An important role all this sneaking around had distracted me from. I found my old school friend reclining on a lounger in the garden.

"You have a lovely place here, Jess. And your Mum is a total star."

The afternoon air squealed in response to the scraping metal legs of my sun lounger as I dragged it across the patio. Snoozing birds of all varieties flapped and squawked their objections to my rude invasion on their afternoon siesta. "Yes, she is. I don't know how she does it all. Do you know where she is now?"

"I think she was heading to the market to get stuff for dinner. You are so lucky, Jess, to have all your family around you."

"I know. I'm still getting used to it all, if I'm honest. But we're family too. You, me, and Sam. The Wesberrey Angels. We're both here for you, no matter what."

Karen rolled over on her side to face me. "I know, but it's not the same, is it? Neither one of you has children, do you? You invested your lives in your careers. I gave mine for Ellen and now she's gone."

Perhaps this was my opening to find out if Ellen was adopted. "It's true I never carried my own child, but Zuzu was always travelling, chasing some new man or other. I was a hands-on aunt to my three nieces when they lived with Mum. I have some idea of your sacrifices."

Karen swung her legs around and bent over on the side of the lounger. "But it's not the same as cooking a new life in your belly," she rubbed her stomach, "and being one with another human being. We were so close when she was little. We did everything together. Then she hit puberty, and everything started to change." *So, Ellen is not little Guenièvre Marron.*

"The teenage years are hard. Children often rebel."

"Teenage years, my arse! That's the priest in you talking. If you had a daughter, you would understand how much it hurts when they don't want you anymore." Karen bit back her tears. "Ellen thought only of herself. I spoiled her and she moved on when I outlived my usefulness. No sugar coating that. It's my fault. I taught her she was special, destined for greatness. The world was hers for the taking. I can't blame her when she went off to claim her birth right, can I?"

"I'm sure she loved you, though. She sounds like she was finding her way in the world, that's all." I thought about all the times I'd screened my mother's calls because I was too busy. I never stopped loving her. "Life overtakes us all at times."

"Death overtakes life," she sobbed.

"Yes, and I know I should tell you it's all part of God's plan, but I can't explain it. We cannot begin to understand his reasons."

"*If* he has any. Jess, I know this is your job, but I'll be honest, I get more comfort from your witchy side."

To be honest, at that very moment, so did I. "Cindy told me that Ellen had one shot to send a message back, and she used that window to tell you she loves you."

Karen grabbed both of my hands and squeezed them. "Yes, she did, didn't she? And she got my gift. I thought she would think it was childish. Ellen was always so serious. So logical. But she loved Britney. My fondest memories are of her dancing to her videos. She knew all the moves." Karen drifted off, humming along to a hazy memory of 'Hit me baby, one more time.'

"And that's how you should remember her." *What if the password was Britney's date of birth?* "Karen, when I went out earlier... I was told that Ellen kept a diary. It's written in code. Would that sound right to you?"

My friend freed a hand to wipe the teardrops from her nose and cheeks. "Ellen was a fiend for puzzles. Word games. Those quest video games. With what's her name? Lara Croft! She made up a secret language when she was twelve. I guess she could still use that, or an updated version of it. Why, do you think they killed her for a diary?"

"I think the diary is the link between her death and the first mate's. It seems he took it but couldn't understand it. I don't suppose you know what that code was?"

"No, I always respected her privacy. If she'd written it in code, then she didn't want me to read it."

"Do you think she would have the key to the code stored on her laptop?" I asked hopefully.

"I doubt it. She knew it off by heart." *Hope dashed.*

*****

I offered to make us both a pitcher of Pimm's and lemonade and took the opportunity to call the inspector with my latest updates. Good to his word, Dave had sent in an officer straight after my earlier call to retrieve the diary. It was already bagged and on its way to the forensics lab in Stourchester. With no evidence to charge anyone, he'd given the rest of the Aurora Agency passes to go into town, or for a walk, etc. They still could not leave the island or return to the yacht.

"Have they hacked Ellen's laptop yet?" I asked.

"No, the date of birth you suggested didn't work."

"That's because Ellen wasn't adopted. But she was a huge Britney Spears fan. Try BJS02121981." *Google is your friend.*

"I'll pass it on. And Jess, thank you for helping us find the diary. You can let it rest, okay? Look after your friend. She needs you to do the day job now."

"I will, just keep me in the loop. I want to find answers for Karen." I wanted to solve the puzzle, and I knew Ellen would want me to as well.

Thoughts raced through my head as I chopped the lemon slices. If she wasn't Celeste's child, then who was? Maybe the birth certificate was a complete red herring, but there was something in Ellen's coded diary that bothered another member of her team enough to kill her and Archie. Something important enough to commit two murders to conceal. *Where are the raspberries?* I pulled out the vegetable tray in the bottom of the fridge. *Oh, there they are, hiding behind the spring onions.* Surely in this enlightened age, having an illegitimate child wasn't so scandalous as to cause someone to kill to keep it a secret? *Now for some ice.* Awkward, embarrassing, unwelcome? Perhaps. A motive for murder? Unlikely.

I had to talk everything through with a brain mightier than my own. Lawrence would provide that wisdom in a few hours. Right now, I needed to get this tray of summery goodness outside without tripping over and sending everything flying.

# School's Out

I took some fresh food and water up to the cemetery for Hugo's girlfriend, Paloma, and her gang of feral felines. The fierce heat of midday had subsided, but most of the cats were still sunning themselves on the ancient headstones. Most of them were too relaxed to notice me refilling their water bowls.

Mission accomplished; I sauntered along the road towards the school yard. There was no hurry. The threatened thunderstorms were nowhere to be seen. The clear blue above was devoid of any clouds, let alone anything menacing and filled with rain. The parched earth beneath my feet would have lapped up any sky offerings. The trees that lined my walk, though, would have to continue their patient vigil, unlike the over excited school children whose voices in the distance trumpeted their wait was done. School was over, for today at least.

I sped up slightly at the sight of Lawrence's blond hair over the black iron railing. If I could catch him before he got back inside the building, I wouldn't need to speak to Audrey, the school receptionist. That woman still gave me the cold shoulder whenever she saw me, which made meeting up with Lawrence at his place of work very unpleasant. As parish priest, I had to visit regularly on parish and personal business and Audrey Matthews never missed an opportunity to place a well-timed cutting remark or jab my way.

I got close enough to grab his trailing wrist just before the reception door. "You need to learn to walk slower," I gasped.

"You could have called out." He smiled and leaned down to kiss me on the cheek.

I knew the colour was rushing to my face. "I didn't want to draw attention." I said, looking around for any straggling parents in the bike shed.

"You know, Jess. This is the worst kept secret on the island. I say we should go public. Put out a notice in the Stourchestershire Times. I can see the headline now." He raised his hand to spell out the title in the sky. "Sexy vicar steals head teacher's heart!"

"Well, you got the vicar bit right." My blush was now down to my toes.

"I have it all right," he countered. "Jess, I know you think I was drunk the other night, but I remember what I said."

"Oh?" *Keep your cool, Jessamy Ward, don't look too eager* "Well, you didn't so..."

"Because, *when* I ask you, I want it to be the most romantic setting possible. Not when I'm still bleary-eyed and chomping down on a bacon butty."

"When?"

*Fiddlesticks! I thought I said that in my head!*

"Yes, sexy vicar. *When.*"

*Cue plump angels with harp music.*

"Mr Pixley, I have the district director on the phone. Shall I tell him you are busy?" Audrey's shrill voice intercepted Cupid's dart.

Lawrence sighed. "Patch him through to my office." And still clasping me close with his cornflower gaze added. "Oh, and could you get some iced tea for Reverend Ward, please? She seems rather hot to me."

\*\*\*\*\*

Hot? I was positively on fire. I would say yes over a bacon butty, or a cheese sandwich or a mouldy slice of bread! His smile filled my veins with lava. Iced tea could not put out this ardour. Watching him skilfully negotiate more funds from the district director for the sports day next week only ramped up the heat. I realised that any hesitation in taking this relationship to the next level rested squarely on my own insecurities. I was a menopausal woman whose prime was ebbing away with each blood-free month and here was a man who thought I was sexy! *Maybe the laser-eye surgery has gone too far?* Jess, stop it! He genuinely cares for you. Enjoy. Smile back. *You are worthy.*

His phone call finished; Lawrence came over to join me on the tattered sofa at the side of his office. I snuggled up against his chest and purred. This was my happy space.

"So, are you going to tell me, what you were doing up at the manor house when you ignored my call?"

"Looking for Ellen Findlay's diary."

"And you did this, why?"

I realised there was a lot to catch him up on. "The police caught Captain Jack this morning. Hold on, let's roll back a little. You have heard that Archie is dead, right?"

"From Audrey 'The island telegraph' Matthews. Yes. But not from you. So, why don't you tell me all about it." He planted a tender kiss on the top of my head. "And don't stop til you get to the bit where you are lying in my arms right now." I was delighted to oblige.

"Then, I fed the cats in the graveyard and the rest you know."

"Hmm, not sure how I feel about another man buying you a double scoop of ice cream. And in public as well. Tongues will wag." I knew he was joking.

"Let them. Audrey already thinks I am a brazen hussy after all the handsome men in Wesberrey. It's the perfect cover. Means no one will suspect the truth."

"And what truth is that, pray tell." His hand stroked my neck.

I tilted my face up to meet his. "That I have fallen deeply in love with the most beautiful headmaster in the kingdom."

"Then you must give me this braggart's name, so I can hunt him down and wrestle him in a duel of wits and cunning."

I ended his quest with my lips.

*****

Fire dampened by a few tender kisses; we picked apart the clues we had. Lawrence uncovered a dusty old blackboard from beyond his filing cabinet and we took a piece of chalk each. I wrote 'Ellen' and circled her name in the centre of the board. Such a mind map had worked well for me before. Lawrence drew spokes radiating out from the circle and together we added the names of the other suspects, including Archie, who I then crossed out.

"I suppose Archie could have killed Ellen when he stole the diary and then whoever asked him to retrieve it killed him afterwards."

"But they didn't get the diary. Seems reckless. You said that you got the feeling that he wasn't murdered." Lawrence passed the chalk stub from hand to hand as he paced beside me.

"If the poolside was wet, then he could have slipped and hit his head on the way down."

"Okay, so let's keep Archie as a suspect in Ellen's death, but accident or not, another person on this blackboard was there when Archie fell into the pool."

"But then why didn't they find the diary?"

"They don't have your sleuthing radar. I wouldn't have thought about checking the shutters," Lawrence squeezed my arm. His pride migrated through my sleeve and into my heart.

"Or they didn't have time?"

"Or the person who was there at his death didn't know about the diary!"

I paused and took a mental snapshot of this incredible conversation. I had found my puzzle partner. We would solve this mystery together in a blaze of chalk dust. "Let's look at each suspect one at a time."

"Right. Let's start with the boss, Steve Huntsford. What do we know about him?"

"He's rich, handsome and totally besotted with his wife of twenty-five years."

"You think he's handsome, eh?" Lawrence nudged my elbow "Bit too old though, don't you think?"

"Rich trumps age, especially in men. I find it refreshing that no one is suggesting that he was having an affair with the younger women."

"No, but Sweetpea," Lawrence took his piece of chalk and ringed Sweetpea's name a couple of times, "she suggested that Celeste and Jenny were sleeping together."

"Which they both vehemently deny." I added, "And, much like the birth certificate, is a lesbian affair really so shocking these days?"

"If your husband is obsessed with you and is the money man behind your real passion, then yes, perhaps that's a motive?"

"Do you think Ellen was blackmailing Celeste? The murderer could be either Jenny or Celeste, or were they acting together?"

"But you said Annie overheard Jenny and Sweetpea talking to Archie. If that was about the diary, then Sweetpea knew too."

"We don't really know anything, do we?" I thudded back down on the sofa.

Lawrence stretched out his arm. "Stop pouting, you can't give up now." I allowed him to pull me back up and drag me to the board. "Back to Steve. Maybe he learnt of Ellen's blackmail attempt and confronted her. He got angry. Rode in on his mythical charger to protect his wife's honour and during the fight pushed his HR Manager overboard."

"There were no signs on the yacht of a struggle. No blood. Nothing was broken."

"Then maybe he rammed her. Ellen was standing on the poop deck, or whatever, facing out to sea, and the murderer seized their opportunity and just ran into her."

"But... then why did her body wash up on the other side of the island? I mean.... Hold on, there's something not right here. Captain Jack said that he laid anchor by Stone Quay and left them to go to the pub. That was on Sunday night. The pub closes at eleven, right? I need to find out when Jack Shipton arrived at the Cat and Fiddle."

"I'm sorry, Jess, my love, you've lost me."

"If Ellen fell overboard in the harbour, surely someone would have seen it or heard the splash? I have fallen in there before and, yes, it's cold and a little choppy but whilst I can see how she could have died if she hit a boat's motor or something, surely her body would have surfaced closer by?"

"So, are you saying that they killed her out at sea?"

"That makes the most sense, doesn't it? To have sustained that much damage to her body. Who has their motors on whilst they are in dock? But wait, no, she was looking at the lights! The fireworks! Lawrence, she died in the harbour.

On Sunday night. The lights were the last thing she saw. How did she drift out to the lighthouse so quickly?"

"You need to talk to Bob. He knows all the tides and currents round here. He would know if it were possible for her to travel that far."

"And I need to talk to Phil and Barbara, find out what time Jack got to the Cat and Fiddle. Before or after the firework display. I'm not sure how that will help, but it seems to be the missing piece of the puzzle."

"One of many," Lawrence smiled. "Now, Reverend Ward, it's getting late. However, I think we still have a few minutes before you have to dash back to the vicarage. I suggest we pick up where we left off earlier."

*Oh, my! Lawrence and Jessie sitting in a tree, K.I.S.S.I.N. G...*

# Forever Friends

I wanted to call Bob's number the moment I stepped off of Cloud Nine, but as I walked through the vicarage door, the sobs emanating from the morning room brought me back with a bump. They say grief comes in waves and Karen was currently wrestling with a tsunami. Questions about tides and currents would need to wait till morning. My friend needed me to be a friend, not a detective.

"Jess, you're back. Where did you go?"

The guilt of spending the last few hours in the arms of love rippled through my response. "I told you, I had to see Lawrence about school business."

Sam appeared at the doorway, steamy mugs of tea in hand. "That's what they are calling it these days, eh?" She placed both cups on coasters on the coffee table and scooted to wrap her long arms around our distraught friend. "She's been like this for an hour. I tried to coax her into eating something, but she can't face it."

"Maybe, she's heard about your cooking? No one should be subjected to that." I wanted to lighten the mood. I couldn't take away Karen's pain, but we could distract her for a while. "Is Mum still out?"

Karen lifted her head from her handkerchief. "Sorry, she called just after you left. Said she was going to her sisters for dinner. Give us some space, you know. She's very kind."

Sam clapped her hands. "Great, well, in that case..." She reached for her bag down at the side of the settee and pulled out a bottle of whiskey. "I think those mugs need a shot of something, don't you?"

"Another present from a grateful patient. You must work miracles in your little hospital."

"Nope, that's your department. I'll have you know that the cupboard is bare. I went into town to buy this one myself."

I hesitated. "Guys don't let me stop you, but I have drunk so much this week. I'll take a pass and find us something to eat. I can just about manage an omelette. Or there are some microwaveable spuds in the freezer."

Karen snorted. "Well, I'll take your share. And a jacket potato sounds good. Do you have any tuna mayonnaise?"

"I should think so." Though being honest, since Mum moved in, I didn't know what there was to eat. It just appeared like magic on the table every night. "Sam, do you want to find a film on Netflix? I say we all get our PJs on and have a sleepover."

Shortly after the last morsel of potato left her plate, Karen nodded off beside me, leaving me and Sam to watch the rest of *An Officer and a Gentleman* alone. Sam tapped my shoulder. "Have you had any more visions?"

"Nope, not a one. Have you heard any more from the coroner's office?"

Sam double-checked Karen was sound asleep. "It looks like Archie Baldwin's death was accidental, unless someone pushed him, of course. But there was no sign of a struggle, and it appears he hit his head on the edge of the pool."

"So, he could have slipped."

"Yes, it's possible.""And..." I mouthed the word 'Ellen', just in case Karen could hear us.

Sam's voice dropped to a whisper. "It's hard to determine, but tests revealed some scorching round her abdomen. The water damage and all the post-mortem bruising made it difficult to see, but the coroner thinks they shot her with a flare."

"Oh no!" I gasped, covering my mouth to muffle the sound. "Then it was murder." *And not just murder, but a violent, horrific end.* "We can't let Karen ever find this out."

Sam stroked our friend's peroxide ponytail. "No, she never needs to know that."

\*\*\*\*\*

Friday morning arrived with a Disney soundtrack. The dawn chorus was accompanying my mother's recital of princess songs to work by. Who knew how much of this impromptu concert I had missed. But now, broadcasting live from the vicarage kitchen, we had 'Part of Your World', from *The Little Mermaid*.

I staggered into the kitchen to find Mum wiping a 'dingle-hopper' with a dishcloth. "Mum, I don't want to rain on your parade, but it's way too early to be singing."

"Sorry, dear, but it is a beautiful day."

I peered through the curtains to the garden outside. "Yes and dazzling already!"

"I'll get you some coffee. Looks like you're going to need it. By the way, don't forget Scissor Sisters at ten."

"Scissor...?" *Our hair appointments!* "Of course, not. How could I forget?" Talking to Bob will have to wait a little longer.

Sam had to skip to the hospital, so Mum and I left a note for Karen to find when she woke up. How she had slept through so far was a mystery, or maybe not - given the circumstances.

As I was expecting to get my hair professionally coiffed, we took the railway down. No outings on Cilla until after the ceremony. Tom and Ernest had the day off, so two teenage volunteers greeted us politely and without fanfare. The young man at the bottom station barely acknowledged our presence. In his defence, the next carload of pretty girls with their short shorts and pastel tops took most of his attention. They were a worthy distraction. Their final school exams had ended the day before. Their last summer together had just begun. Their excitement was palpable. The island would be host to these fresh, adolescent dreams for the next eight weeks. It was the same every year past and would be so for many years to come. Time marches on. The wheel turns. Birth, life, and death - the cycle continues. Everything changes, yet everything stays the same.

\*\*\*\*\*

It was only a little after nine when we reached Market Square. Still plenty of time to get to our appointment. I thought if I was quick, I could grab a few words with Bob before he took out the next ferry. I promised Mum I would be at the hairdressers in good time and pushed my way through the growing morning crowd. The Regatta was drawing to a close, and the street was heaving with tourists.

Bob was collecting tickets on the jetty, but the queue was longer than usual, and I knew he would be in no mind to stand and chat. I pressed on towards the *Norma Jean* instead. The Captain might have a few answers to my questions. I found him literally mopping the decks.

"Morning, Vicar, Thought I get her Bristol fashion whilst I'm land bound."

There was no sign of his police guard. "Where's the fuzz? I thought Inspector Lovington had you under boat arrest?"

"They're both in the galley, getting some breakfast. Nice chaps, for coppers."

"Well, I suppose you can't run without the keys."

Captain Jack leaned to rest on his mop. "Just shows how stupid that Errol Flynn look-a-like is then, Vicar. Like I would only have one set of keys."

*How stupid of me, too!* "So where are the others?"

"I have a few sets hidden, and of course there are the masters in the cockpit. Pirates." he huffed, "Never can be too careful."

"Do you get many pirates in the charter business?"

"You'd be surprised. There's a lot of wealth on these condomarans."

"I suppose so. Have you noticed any of the keys are missing?"

"Nope, but then I'll be honest, I haven't looked. By the way, I hear you found the diary. What did you make of it?"

"Not much. I took some photos but haven't really scrutinized them. You were right though, it's all in gobble-de-gook."

"My question would be, not that anyone would ask me," Jack grunted, "what things do people want to hide?"

"Things they want to remain secret." I flipped on my phone.

"Exactly, and most secrets are about sex or money. That lot are as open as a raided treasure chest about sex, so I say - follow the money."

"And money would point to Steve or Celeste?"

Jack shrugged and plunged the mop into the grey bucket at his feet. My audience was over, and I had an appointment to make.

# Hair Today, Gone Tomorrow

T he ferry was out when I got back to the port, but I didn't really have time to spare. I couldn't be late for Barbara's surprise hen party. Well, maybe only by a few minutes. Ten. Max.

Okay, fifteen. Mum scowled at me as I entered Scissor Sisters. I had missed the big 'Surprise!' moment. Zuzu spotted the need for an intervention and whisked me off to the back of the salon.

"Jessie! Come on, this is Barbara's big day. And she's more your friend than ours."

"Oh really? Now she's my friend, yet you all have been privy to the dress and the decorations, and I'm relegated to the church stuff."

"We all have our specialisms," Zuzu replied, covering her hand to mask her giggles at my fake offence. *The cake! I never asked Rosie about the cake!*

"I forgot to ask. You have sorted the wedding cake, right?"

Zuzu patted my shoulder and guided me to a couple of chairs in the waiting area. "Oh, ye of little faith. Rosie has it all in hand. Relax and join in the fun. Okay? Tea, coffee, champagne?"

"Tea, thank you." Scissor Sisters was jumping. Music poured from the wall mounted speakers. Junior stylists served trays of canapes. And the twins, Verity and Avril, fussed over their guest of honour. Barbara was loving every minute.

The shop bell tinkled to announce another visitor, and Mandy McGuire rushed in with her cherubic youngest child in a pushchair. "Oh, I'm sorry," she shouted over the music. "I didn't realise you were having a party. I wanted to see if you could fit me in for a last-minute cut and blow dry." Dwayne, the twins' top stylist, whisked her into a vacant chair beside me and thrust some magazines in her hand.

"If you're prepared to wait, my love, I'll do you after the Reverend here." Dwayne snapped his perfectly manicured fingers to summon food and drinks.

Mandy was Bob's younger sister, and I knew her from our weekly Wesberrey Walkers workouts. I never really had much opportunity to speak with her. She was always rushing hither and thither after her four children. All born out of wedlock, but as Our Lord said, he who is without sin, etc.

"Is this your youngest? What's her name?"

"Melody." Mandy pulled a baby wipe out of a plastic pouch at the side of her buggy and attempted to clean up her daughter's chubby fingers.

"What a lovely name. Are the others at school? I think I have met your eldest, Charlie? He is very vocal during assembly."

Mandy unwrapped a rusk biscuit and wedged it into Melody's eager hand. "Yep, that sounds like my Charlie. Always has something to say for himself."

"He's a clever lad. And you have two more?" I was keen to maintain small talk. Dwayne was currently working his magic on my sister, Rosie. I was far down the line.

"Yes, four, for my sins. You'd think I'd have worked out how it happens by now." She smiled. "Melody will be my last. But I've said that every time."

I smiled back. "And you all live with your brother. That must be nice. Having him around."

"Yeah, Bob's a veritable saint, Reverend. Not sure how I would manage without him. Is that your sister in the chair?"

"Rosie? Yes."

"Ah, so that's Rosina Bailey. My brother's carried a torch for her for over thirty years. She split from her husband recently, right?"

Vague memories of a young Bob McGuire pulling my sister's pigtails in class and making her cry rushed into my mind. "Er, yes."

A scream sliced through the air. Verity and Avril were huddled over the bride-to-be, who was wailing hysterically. I had never seen my parish secretary like this. Something must be very wrong. I made my excuses to Mandy and rushed to Barbara's side.

"They promised!" she cried. "What are we going to do now?"

"Who promised? What's up?" I asked Verity, who was battling with the extension wire of a pink hairdryer.

"The police have just called her and said she can't have the pub's reception room back."

I looked at my family, but the solution was obvious. "Then we move everything to the church hall. Right?" Everyone agreed. "Zuzu, sweet talk Dave to let us in to gather up the drapes and the lights. And catering, Rosie. What are you going to cook? Can we do it in the hall kitchen? If not, we could spill over to the vicarage?"

"Jess, the Old School House is doing the heavy lifting. I'm just coordinating. I'm sure they will be happy with the change in venue. The church is closer." *Hmm, French cuisine, very fancy. I really was out of the loop.*

"Right, we have a plan then." I knelt down to comfort my friend. "See, Barbara - all sorted. Verity? Avril. More champagne!"

*****

Mum was next up to the main chair. Barbara joined Mandy and me in the waiting area whilst her blonde dye took. Crisis averted. She was having the time of her life. "This is such a pleasant surprise. I am so blessed and to-morrow, I can't believe it, but I am going to marry the most amazing man in the world!"

Everyone with a drink in their hands, and that was almost everyone, cheered.

"When did you decide to go with the chefs at the Old School House?" I asked. "I must have missed that memo."

"Your sisters suggested it. Phil has never been there because he's always working. I thought it would be a nice treat and you only do this once, eh, Reverend? It's worth doing it right."

We clinked glasses. "Indeed, it is."

"I have the menu here, somewhere." Barbara motioned to Mandy to pass across a large straw basket style handbag with coloured straw flowers near the braided handle mounts. Baby Melody reached out to grab the beaded tassels as it floated in front of her pushchair, caught the longest strand, and put the beaded end straight into her mouth.

Mandy wrestled it away. "I'm so sorry. Here."

"Thank you. It's such a cute age. You have to watch them like a hawk, don't you? Coochie-coochie, coochie-coochie coo!" Barbara tickled Melody's dribbling chin. "Is she teething? Bless her heart." Barbara waved the bag in my general direction. "The menu's inside, it's all in French, so I'm not sure what we'll end up eating."

I balanced my glass in one hand and rummaged through the straw bag with the other. "Rosie, do you know what they've ordered?" I called across to my sister, whose brunette tresses were in the final primping stages.

"Verrines de tartare de saumon fumé et mousse de homard for starters." She replied without having to refer to the menu. *Impressive!*

"See! What's that when it's at home?" giggled Barbara. "I can't even say it!"

Rosie turned her head, frustrating Dwayne's finishing touches. "It's basically smoked salmon and lobster mousse. A very light first course."

"Sounds delicious. I'm sure it will be wonderful." I replied, waving my fingers in a circular motion to encourage Rosie to face the mirror again. "Dwayne needs your head back."

Mandy was trying her best to keep her daughter amused with a wooden rattle. "Everything is more exotic in French. The English versions sound so dull."

They do indeed. Take our mysterious Guenièvre Marron. What would the anglicised version of her name be? My hand trembled as I leaned to set my glass down on the table nearby. It couldn't be, could it? *Jess - you are a complete idiot! Guenièvre Marron is Jenny Brown!*

\*\*\*\*\*

I was next up to sit under Dwayne's magic hands. My instructions to him, though, were vague. *How did I not spot it before?* My mind was racing with the realisation that Jenny was Celeste's daughter. This torrent of thoughts left little room for thinking about hair styles.

"A bob, like before. Toffee Latte was the colour I think."

"Do you want to try anything more daring? Asymmetric, perhaps? Shaved? Or we could run an iced blue through the layers. Or some violet, perhaps? I think that would look great with your skin tone."

I nodded absentmindedly. Dwayne squealed and ran off to the storeroom. I barely noticed he had gone. *If Jenny is Celeste's daughter, that explains their close relationship. It doesn't explain why Ellen wound up dead... Or how she ended up on the beach?*

"Barbara?" I rolled my chair over to the waiting area "Did you see Captain Jack Shipton from the *Norma Jean*, in the Cat and Fiddle on Sunday night?"

"That miserable soak?" Barbara answered between canapes "Yes, he was there, Reverend, moaning about the fireworks."

"So, that puts him there about, what? Nine-thirty? Ten?"

"Yes, I guess so. Because of the kiddies we usually set them off just after it goes dark."

"So, that means that the *Norma Jean* was in the harbour before nine."

"I suppose so."

"But she wasn't." Mandy piped in. "Bob saw her rounding the headland on his final crossing. That would have been around half ten."

"He what? Has he told the police?" This additional information ricocheted around my brain like a squash ball.

Mandy looked puzzled. "I think so. I don't know. I mean, he can't have done, if the captain was in the pub, can he?" *Unless someone else took the yacht out!*

"Is your brother sure he saw the *Norma Jean* that night?"

"Yes, he was talking about it this morning. He didn't pay it much mind till they made it public that the girl was on-board that particular yacht. I mean, he thought it strange at the time, but didn't connect the dots. Most of the boats stay close to shore after dark."

I wanted to ask more questions, but Dwayne dragged my chair back to his station.

"Right, Reverend, let's play!"

# Teamwork

I was desperate to relay all this new information to the police, but I was in the chair and couldn't go anywhere for a good hour or so. There is a powerful school of thought that urges one to focus on the now. To stay mindful and appreciate the present. Perhaps, if I'd done that rather than filled my head with crazy murder plots. Or not frantically searched the web on my phone for clues to Ellen's or Archie's pasts. I would have noticed the strange colour of the dye mix in the plastic bucket Dwayne was holding. And I may have been aware that he was sectioning off my hair and applying a different shade to certain parts. But I didn't. I was too immersed in the quest to find any trace of Ellen Findlay on social media.

"Ooh, so brave?"

"I love it!"

"That really suits you, Reverend,"

"Jessamy Ward! What have you done?"

The last comment was from my mother. *Always a fan!*

"Seriously Jessie, I adore it! Dwayne, you are a genius!" Zuzu twirled me around for all to see. "You look ten years younger."

The chair came to a halt in front of the gilded mirror. Dwayne stood behind me, beaming with pride. "Well? What do you think?" He held up a smaller second mirror to show me the back. My reflection showed that he had cut the back into a graduated bob over two layers. The top was a warm brown, the bottom a cobalt blue. The back looked gorgeous. I wasn't sure it matched my middle-aged face.

*Jess, you have envied such courageous choices on others. Embrace it. Smile! It will grow out!* "It's lovely. Thank you."

\*\*\*\*\*

The hen party, freshly beautified and giddy on canapes and champagne, headed to the Cat and Fiddle to reclaim the decorations and begin the move to the church hall. It would have been rude to abandon the group now, though I was hoping for a few minutes' grace to update the inspector.

Fortunately, Zuzu made the necessary introductions. "Dave, what do you think of Jessie's cool new look?"

"Em, it's, er, interesting. No offence, ladies, but this is a working incident room. Can you get everyone in and out as soon as possible?"

"Ooh, someone's feeling the pressure." Zuzu walked her fingers up his shirt buttons. "I know just the cure for that. But business first." She kissed the Baron on the cheek and flounced off to join the clacking hens pulling down the white curtains.

I lingered to share the latest updates gleaned from my conversation at the salon. "So, I think they sailed out again, using one of the spare keys, to dump Ellen's body out to sea. They just didn't reckon on the current washing her ashore so quickly."

"Great work. And thank you for bringing it straight to me. I appreciate that."

"A promise is a promise. No more detecting for me." I paused. "But if we could crack the code in the diary. I know that would explain everything. Did your team open the laptop?"

"They did, Britney Spears was a good guess,"

"Inspired, I think you meant to say, but thank you." I itched to get more intel. "And?"

"And?" *Man, he was insufferable!*

"And what did they find?"

Dave's tell-tale twitch worked overtime. "That, *Reverend* Ward, is police business."

"Oh, Dave, come on." I stamped my foot. "I have given you so much. You would never have learnt that Jenny was Celeste's daughter without me. You now have another red-hot lead, right? That has to have scored me some brownie points?"

"Yes, I will give you that. You have been very helpful. But a deal is a deal. Brownie's honour, remember? You have acted as any good citizen would. Now be a good friend." He cricked his neck, planted both hands on my shoulders and turned me towards my friends at the far end of the room. "You have plenty to keep you busy."

*Uh-huh, hold it right there.* I pivoted back again. "Just tell me, did they find the key to the code used in the diary?"

"No, nothing. It was full of work stuff. Emails, excel sheets, reports. Nothing personal at all."

"Don't you think that's strange? We didn't even find a mobile. No Instagram, no Facebook? Look." I got out my phone and searched for Ellen Findlay on Google. "She's like a ghost!" *Poor choice of words.*

Dave grabbed the phone from my hand. "I knew it! You can't help yourself. What else do you have on here?" He scrolled through my apps and landed on my snaps of the diary.

"I can explain."

"Jess, please. I have to delete these."

"No, you don't." I protested. "We can crack the code together. We're missing something. Her phone is probably at the bottom of the channel, but there's something old-school about having a paper diary, don't you think?" Dave stroked his moustache. I knew it intrigued him. "Look, the way I see it, there are several possibilities here. What we don't have is motive. The diary could give us that." *It's now or never.* "First, who sailed the *Norma Jean* out again Sunday night? I assumed Archie was talking about the diary when he said to the girls 'have you got my back on this', but he could have been referring to the late-night cruise."

Dave reached into his breast pocket and got out his notebook. "Go on."

"Or it could have been Steve Huntsford, right? We know he can sail. But what motive would either man have? Either they killed Ellen, or they were helping the person who did. The killer shot Ellen with a flare gun, so..."

"Hold on, how did you know that?"

"I have my sources." *Don't stop now, he's hooked.* "Steve would do anything to protect his wife. Celeste would have grounds to be angry with Ellen if she were trying to blackmail her over Jenny's parentage. Or maybe it was Jenny herself. It could have been a row that got out of hand. Perhaps Sweetpea was a witness and the young women panicked and roped in poor Archie to help them?"

"But at least one of them asked Archie to steal the diary, so regardless of who sailed the yacht that night, that person knew of its existence and wanted the evidence to disappear." Dave flicked back and forth through his notebook, looking for any clues.

"Or the two things are unconnected. Without breaking the code, we will never know."

"Okay, okay. So, do you have any idea how we can go about breaking the code? Maybe something her mother has told you?"

"Karen hasn't said much, to be honest. Ellen was a fan of Britney Spears, Lara Croft and puzzles."

"Tomb Raider? Okay. That might be useful, I'll get the team on it."

"There has to be something in her belongings. That bed was... Jenny!" *Jess, where did you leave your brain? On cloud nine with lovely Lawrence, that's where!* "Jenny's room at the manor. She made her bed the same way. I mean, Archie didn't make Ellen's bed. Jenny did."

"So, Ellen was blackmailing Jenny. They fought. Jenny shot off the flare and then dragged Archie in on it. Got him to sail out the yacht after hours and steal the diary. That's plausible."

"It all works, but why? If Celeste already knew Jenny was her daughter, and their close relationship would suggest she did, what could Ellen have been blackmailing Jenny about?"

"Perhaps this has nothing to do with her birth mother." Dave suggested. "There's another reason."

"And I'm sure the diary holds the key."

The rest of the group was getting ready to leave. Zuzu returned to claim her man. "Seriously, a girl could get jealous," she joked. "Jess, if I can drag you away, we have a lot of work to do to get everything ready for tomorrow. You were moaning earlier about being out of the loop.

Well, now's your chance. Rosie has to get back to the shop. Seems she is expecting a delivery of steamy romances for the top shelf and doesn't want Luke to open the boxes. I told her to put a couple by for me. Bedtime reading for when lover boy here is on duty." She threw a seductive wink towards the inspector that he was clearly excited to cash in later.

"Bedtime reading?" *That's it!* "Rosie, I don't suppose you have a copy of *How To Win Friends and Influence People?*" I shouted across the room.

Dave snapped back from whatever fantasy Zuzu had inspired this time. "The book by her bed!"

"And the markings that were in it. My money's on that being the key to the code."

# What Would Poirot Do?

Ellen's copy of the book was filed as evidence back at the Stourchester police headquarters. Dave put in a call for it and the diary to be dispatched as soon as possible.

"Again, Jess, thank you for your help. But I can take it from here."

"We could pop to the shop and see if Rosie has a copy?" I was so close to unravelling it all. I wanted desperately to be there at the end. My poker face must have slipped - a little.

"Don't pull that look with me, Jess. Even if your sister has a copy gathering dust somewhere, it's not Ellen's copy.

Come on, this was fun, but enough is enough. Leave it to the professionals, namely me, okay? Now, off you go." *Grrr, why don't you just pat me on the head and say I'm a good girl? Woof, woof!*

I grabbed a box of fairy lights. Kicking my heels, I followed the other women through the main bar. Inside the pub, it was easy to forget that the sun blazed outside. The cobbled square quivered from the heat. I stopped to survey the scene. Lots of people, young and old, enjoying the gift of being alive on this beautiful day. A gift someone had denied my friend's only daughter. *Promise or no promise. I can't step away now.*

I wandered away from the group and headed to Dungeons and Vegans.

\*\*\*\*\*

I arrived at the bookshop just as Rosie was signing for her steamy delivery.

"Jess? You're supposed to be with the others?"

I placed the fairy lights on one of the cafe tables. "I know, But I can't. Not until I try one last thing. Please, little

Sis, do you have a copy of that book stashed in the back somewhere?"

Rosie agreed to look if I helped her with the boxes now piled on the pavement outside her store. They were heavy, but my reward was a dusty volume of *How To Win Friends and Influence People.* It was an early edition, with a black and white dust cover featuring a picture of Dale Carnegie himself on the jacket. And was nothing like the one Ellen owned.

"Do you have any other copies? A paperback maybe?"

"No, Jess, I looked. I don't get why it's important."

"Because we need to crack the code!" I spluttered, my frustration rising. I wanted to catch Ellen's killer. I owed it to my friend. Then I would step away.

"Well, maybe there's more than one way to skin a cat?"

"What do you mean?"

"Well, you could go all Hercule Poirot on the suspects and see which one of them breaks?"

"Or the answer might come to me as I talk!"

"Yes, well, that too, I suppose."

"Rosie, you're a genius." I grabbed the box of fairy lights. "Oh, and by the way, the tables look great!

*****

I hailed one of Wesberrey's finest horse-drawn hackney carriages "To Bridewell Manor, please!" He dropped me off at the gate. The gravel under my feet, as I slogged up to the main house, felt like quicksand in the heat. I wasn't sure my heart would make it. Panting for breath, I rang the doorbell.

"Ralph, is Lady Arabella in?" I gasped.

"Yes, Reverend. She is holding court with all her guests in the lounge. Can I get you anything? A glass of water, perhaps? Or a fan?"

"The heart of a twenty-two-year-old?"

"Sorry, we're all out of them." He held out his hands to relieve me of the fairy lights.

"Thank you. Shall I just go through?"

"Unless you want me to announce you?"

"Ooh, yes, that would be fun. Quick question. Where are the police? I thought everyone was still on semi-house arrest?"

"Two officers are hanging out with us in the pantry. It's nice to have the company."

"Great." I winked, "We might need them later."

Ralph placed the box on a side table and strode towards the sitting room doors. "Reverend Ward to see you, your ladyship."

I bowed my gratitude and, head held high, I walked towards the surprised looks of the assembled party.

Arabella greeted me with outstretched arms. "Jess, how wonderful. I hope you haven't come back for that swim. We're having the pool drained right now."

"No, maybe another time. I actually wanted to speak to your guests, if I may?"

"The floor is all yours, Reverend."

The first burst of bravado that carried me through the door was morphing into quiet panic. *Act like you know more than you do!* I paced the room as I talked, observed people's reactions, and adjusted my narrative accordingly. My earlier training as an actress would be put fully to the test.

"Thank you, Lady Somerstone-Wright. I am delighted that you are all here. It will make what I have to say so much easier." *If only I knew what that was...*

Steve Huntsford had been reading the Financial Times in a wingback chair in the corner. "Speak up then, Reverend. Ralph should be on his way soon with afternoon tea."

"I promise, I won't keep you too long." I took a calming breath. "It's just. You see. My old school friend, Karen. Well, her daughter was, it turns out, Ellen Findlay. Which in itself is a remarkable coincidence. One way or another, I have been involved in this tragic case since early Monday morning. Or rather, I suppose what remained of Sunday night."

Jenny, sat beside Celeste on the sofa, also steadied herself with a deep, measured breath before speaking. "We all know that Reverend Ward, but what exactly has brought you here today?"

"Ellen's killer. You see, I think I know who it is!"

The gasp from the room was not as dramatic as I expected. In fact, it wasn't so much a gasp as a gentile sip of air. The fact that I had absolutely no idea who the killer was would not stop me. There were two ways this would go, and I was determined that the final scenario would not leave me with the proverbial egg on my face. *Have faith!*

"Let's start with the facts, as I see them. Ellen Findlay was shot with a flare by someone in this room on Sunday evening during the fireworks display." The word 'flare' got a response; it was clearly news to some of the group.

"Then that person, or their associate, took a spare set of keys and sailed the *Norma Jean* out to the other side of the island in an attempt to get rid of her body. They probably hoped that would gain them some time. However, the current brought poor Ellen ashore before her murderer had a chance to sound the alarm later that morning. The discovery bringing Inspector Lovington on board and trapping the murderer first on the *Norma Jean* and then here at Bridewell Manor."

Sweetpea, previously slouched across her armchair, straightened up to fiddle with her wig. "The heat today is playing havoc with my hairnet, you know. Sorry, Vicar, you were saying?"

Jenny's anxious eyes pleaded with the room. "I raised the alarm. But I didn't kill Ellen. I didn't. Maman?" She turned to Celeste. "You must believe me."

"Ah, yes, I assume everyone here knows that Jenny is Celeste's daughter?" *Thank you, Jenny, you made that revelation very easy!*

"She's what?" Sweetpea tugged more aggressively at her hair.

"Oh, yes. Jenny Brown here was born Guenièvre Marron. Such a pretty name. Why did you change it?"

Celeste reached over to take her daughter's hand. "I can answer that. Because the orphanage moved her to England. There was the chance of a family here for her, but it fell through. Ma petite fille, je suis tellement désolé. Je n'avais aucune idée. Forgive me."

"How could you know?" Jenny cradled her weeping mother. "Happily, fate brought us back together."

"Oui, and it was Ellen who uncovered the truth. How she worked out that this amazing, beautiful child is my Guenièvre? Mon Dieu, I owe her everything." Celeste fought back the tears. "I would never have hurt her. Never."

"I believe you. Ellen was good at discovering people's secrets. She loved puzzles. And as the HR director, she had access to everyone's personal files."

Pink wig now clenched between two fists on her lap, Sweetpea demanded more information from her boss. "So, you had no idea Jenny was your daughter when you hired her? I find that hard to believe!"

"C'est un miracle, n'est-ce pas." Celeste reinforced her grip on Jenny's hand. "So, naturally, we had DNA tests. The results only came through last week. Steve and I are so happy. What could be better? All my girls are like family. Now, one of them actually is. Reverend, as you say, Dieu se déplace de manière mystérieuse. God, he moves in mysterious ways."

Sweetpea's cheeks grew as crimson as her lipstick. "I can't believe it! Family? When were you going to tell me, eh? Seems like I was the only one who knew nought about it, you know."

"We were going to make an announcement later in the week." Steve folded his paper purposefully, and placing it under his arm, walked over to join his wife on the settee. "Reverend, impressive. How did you work all this out?"

"Ellen left behind a diary. The police have it. It's written in code. Ellen obviously was a very secretive woman. However, we have the key, and they are working through it as we speak."

Jenny looked puzzled. "You have her diary? How? Archie..."

"Archie, what? Jenny, did you ask Archie to steal her diary?"

"No, well, not just me. I mean," Jenny glowered at her hair-netted colleague. "You said it was a bit of fun!" Sweetpea stared angrily back. "That you were going to put it back!"

*Sweetpea! It all made sense now.*

"But you couldn't put it back because you knew Ellen was dead. Isn't that right, Sweetpea? You couldn't take the risk that your DNA or fingerprints would end up in Ellen's room. You shot Ellen Findlay with the flare during the fireworks on Sunday night, and you convinced poor Archie to take the boat out again. Did he know what you had done?"

"You have no proof of anything! What would be my motive, eh? I'm not another of Celeste's bastards, you know!"

*Captain Jack said, if it's not sex, it's money. Follow the money!*

"No, but..." *Time for a leap of faith.* "She found out you were embezzling funds from Aurora, didn't she?"

Her face confirmed I was right. The conversation in the toilet during the dinner party flooded back. Ellen was asking too many questions.

"You told me yourself that she was the crazy bitch from HR, always... what were your exact words? Ah, yes, 'sneaking around' and 'constantly up in everyone's businesses.

The diary will prove it, won't it, that you were subcontracting work to freelancers that didn't exist?"

As I spoke, everything fell into place. *I am on a roll!* "Ellen probably ran background checks on all Aurora's employees. That's how she found out about you, Jenny. She read your birth certificate and her imagination filled in the blanks. Karen told me how much she loved a puzzle. She really was good at her job. She went over and above what we would normally expect in that role. That's why you employed her, Celeste. Because she was the best. Her talent for unmasking corporate rogues and business traitors, got her killed."

Sweetpea readjusted her wig and smoothed down her dress. "You have nothing. No murder weapon. No evidence. So, what if she was mouthing off saying I was skimming a bit off the top? Doesn't mean I silenced her permanently, you know. As you said, there's no DNA evidence. I never went into her room."

"No, you were very clever. You trusted that job to Archie. He stole the diary and then later that evening you met up with Ellen and bang! The fireworks covered the shot. But where was Archie?"

I turned to Jenny. She hung her head. "He was with me."

"And Celeste? Where were you during the fireworks?"

"Steve and I were in bed. We told the Inspector this already."

Steve drew his wife and stepdaughter close. "Yes, the fireworks would have made Celeste's headache worse. We'd knocked back a few whiskeys and were dead to the world by nine. Sorry."

"So, Sweetpea, no witnesses. You orchestrated everything brilliantly. You had been to the Regatta before. You knew Steve and Celeste would retire early. And, of course, this was her first time on the yacht. Ellen would want to watch the fireworks. Keeping Archie and Jenny busy gave you the perfect opportunity to get her on deck alone. You just needed to dispose of her body before everyone woke. How did you get Archie to sail back out? Did you offer him a share? Maybe his own boat? He couldn't be the entertainment forever."

"You're saying I killed him as well? Anyone else? I didn't, you know."

"No, I believe you. People heard you messing around at the pool earlier that night. You were there with Jenny. Just three young people having fun. I think you expected Archie to bring the diary with him that night to the pool. But he'd realised by then how important it was. Ingenious bringing Jenny in on this. You got her to check on Ellen in the morning as well, didn't you?"

Jenny went to speak, but I raised my hand. "I know you were there. You made the bed. You couldn't help but tidy up, could you?"

Jenny sunk back into her mother's embrace. I returned to Sweetpea. "Then you met up again with Archie later to renegotiate your deal. But he wanted more money, or something else you'd promised and you, you betrayed him. Didn't you? Rather than retaliate, he turned to walk away and fell. Hitting his head." Sweetpea puffed herself up and slow-clapped me as I talked, but I had more to say. "And the worse bit is, that you could have saved him. He drowned because you let him die."

"You really have quite the imagination there, Vicar!" Sweetpea remained peacock proud in her seat.

"But it's true. You asked Archie to steal the diary. You made a point of getting him to sleep with Ellen that night, when it was your turn. Then you encouraged me to keep him occupied later. You said how much fun it would be to... you know, with the fireworks going off... You made me a part of it." Jenny shuddered. "I made her bed. And she was dead!" Jenny's breathing grew faster and more laboured with every word. "And Archie! When you told me to close my eyes and run into the pool. You *knew* he was in there!"

Arabella rang the bell to summon Ralph. "I think we have heard more than enough. Tea can wait. It's time to call in the police."

# Marry When June Roses Grow

S aturday morning brought a flurry of activity to the main church and the church hall. After the drama of Friday afternoon, it was all hands-on deck to prepare the hall for the wedding reception. Inspector Lovington had arrested Sweetpea Smythe and charged her with the murder of Ellen Findlay and the manslaughter of Archie Baldwin. The boffins back at the lab at Stourchester police station eventually deciphered the Carnegie Code later that evening. Ellen's diary contained details of offshore bank accounts and falsified records under Sweetpea's watch going back over two years. She had successfully embezzled over three-quarters of a million pounds.

"Imagine not knowing you were short by a million quid?" Rosie handed me some green foliage to wind around a glass lantern on the table setting I was working on. "But then, that wouldn't buy you much these days. A small flat in London, perhaps."

"I think that's why Celeste recruited her. Though you could get a castle in Scotland with that money." I wrapped the stem around the neck of an empty jar destined to be a candle holder.

"True. I know which I would prefer." Rosie wiped some loose orange blossom buds from the tablecloth and stood back to admire all our hard work. "I think it looks beautiful, Jess. I meant to ask, what is Karen planning to do today? I am sure Barbara would be fine with her coming to the reception. There's plenty of food and I can squeeze in an extra chair."

"Way ahead of you, little Sis, but she is heading over to the funeral home to talk to Leo about arrangements. I think she wants some time alone."

We gathered up the rest of the decorations. "I'll whizz over after the ceremony to light the candles. The chef needs access to the kitchen from about one. So, if you leave me with the keys, I can let them in."

"My pleasure. Rosie. Just a thought, what if they don't like French food? Unchartered territory all this posh nosh."

"I've got it covered. They are making some English grub as well."

"You have thought of everything."

"Naturally. Just one more thing. Can you help me with the seating plan?"

I nodded, and we walked together to the storeroom. "That is so pretty. Where am I sitting?"

"On the top table, Barbara insisted." Gratitude and pride sought release through the water droplets that pricked the corners of my eyes. This was not a day for non-waterproof mascara.

I scanned the board. "And there you are. And Luke, Tilly. Oh, and Buck is next to you. Is he your 'plus one'?"

"Maybe," she smiled.

\*\*\*\*\*

Clouds threatened, distant thunder roared, but nothing could darken the radiant vision in white that walked down the centre aisle of St. Bridget's as the church bells tolled three o'clock.

Such was the magnificence of her entrance, Barbara required two handsome men to give her away. Tom and Ernest were the proudest 'fathers' a girl could ask for. Phil, equally resplendent in his light grey three-piece suit with a pale orange cravat and matching silk waistcoat, waited patiently at the foot of the altar steps. His toes tapping to the beat of the *Wedding March* the only show of nerves.

Barbara beamed at every pew, now trimmed with orange blossom and sprigs of baby's breath, greeting all her guests. This was her moment and no one and nothing was going to rush her. Rosemary had to repeat the March several times to cover Barbara's majestic progress through the church. The whole of Wesberrey was there to see their queen finally marry her prince, and the general sighs of approval marked her dress as a triumph.

Sometimes in our lives our hearts brim with so much joy, there is no room left for pain or doubt. The shared mood is of such exquisite perfection, it unites everyone present.

It is in these moments I believe God steps forward. His light. His eternal truth shines in and through us all.

I offered a prayer of thanks. Before me stood two souls entwined in love, who would soon be bound together for all eternity.

As the last chords of the organ died away, I took their hands and began.

"Dearly beloved, we are gathered together here in the sight of God, and in the face of this congregation, to join together this Man and this Woman in holy Matrimony..."

*****

Mr and Mrs Phil Vickers emerged from the dark church into the full glare of the June sun. The earlier showers had brought freshness to the air and lightness to the birdsong that serenaded the newlyweds as they posed for photos in the arched doorway. Confetti trailed down the stone pathways, gathering on the ancient ridges and gullies that lined our route to the hall.

I watched. I waited. I drew in the sweet scent of this happiest of days.

A slender arm weaved its way around my waist. Warm breath caressed my neck. A soft jaw, with the merest hint of stubble, nuzzled my ear. "It's tempting," his gentle voice whispered. "But still not romantic enough."

I tilted my head. The expectant grin on my face drew power from the glow in my chest. "Right now, would be perfect." I replied.

Lawrence spun me around and balanced my chin on the tips of his fingers. His lips melted into mine. "I will wait until we have moonlight, and Paris and a jazz piano."

I pulled back. "Jazz? Now that may be a deal breaker!"

# What's Next for Reverend Jess?

## VESTRY VICE

**Murder in a remote island parish ought to be rare**

...Knee-deep in offerings for the harvest festival and battling the bellringers who appear to be on strike, another mystery is the last thing Jess needs.

However, when the latest body is discovered, it coincides with the arrival of a film crew looking to make a documentary about the now-famous sleuthing vicar. Worse yet, the TV people are led by an old flame.

Unexpectedly at the centre of her own true crime story, all she really wants to do is hide away with a pumpkin-spiced latte. Her cosy night by the fire will have to wait though. There's a killer at large.

Add to the mix some clumsy attempts at courting from the school headmaster and more convincing romantic overtures from the handsome blast from the past and Jess is going to have her work cut out solving this one.

# About the Author

P enelope lives on an island off the coast of Kent, England, with her four children and an elderly Jack Russell Terrier. A lover of murder mystery and cups of tea (served with a stack of digestive biscuits), she writes quaint cosy mysteries and other feel-good stories from a corner table in the vintage tea shop on the high street. Penelope loves nostalgia and all things retro. Her taste in music is also very last century.

Find out more about Penelope at www.penelopecress.com.

# Want to know more?

Greenfield Press is the brainchild of bestselling author Steve Higgs. He specializes in writing fast paced adventurous mystery and urban fantasy with a humorous lilt. Having made his money publishing his own work, Steve went looking for a few 'special' authors whose work he believed in.

Georgia Wagner was the first of those, but to find out more and to be the first to hear about new releases and what is coming next, you can join the Facebook group by copying the following link into your browser - www.facebook.co m/GreenfieldPress.

PENELOPE CRESS, STEVE HIGGS

# Free Books and More

Want to see what else I have written? Go to my website.

https://stevehiggsbooks.com/

Or sign up to my newsletter where you will get sneak peeks, exclusive giveaways, behind the scenes content, and more. Plus, you'll be notified of Fan Pricing events when they occur and get exclusive offers from other authors because all UF writers are automatically friends.

Copy the link carefully into your web browser.

https://stevehiggsbooks.com/newsletter/

Prefer social media? Join my thriving Facebook community.

Want to join the inner circle where you can keep up to date with everything? This is a free group on Facebook where you can hang out with likeminded individuals and enjoy discussing my books. There is cake too (but only if you bring it).

https://www.facebook.com/groups/1151907108277718

Printed in Great Britain
by Amazon

41408824R00155